GW00670563

Summer in the Country

THE SCARLET LIBRARY
LONDON MMI

THE SCARLET LIBRARY

is an imprint of
THE *Erotic* Print Society
EPS, 1 Maddox Street
LONDON W1S 2PZ

Tel (UK only): 0800 026 25 24
Fax: +44 (0)20 7437 3528
Email: *eros@eps.org.uk*
Web: *www.scarletlibrary.com*
OR *www.eroticprints.org*

ISBN: 1-898998-33-7

© 2001 MacHo Ltd, London UK

Summer in the Country

AUGUSTE POULET-MALASSIS
translated by
Terry Hale

with new
illustrations by

ADRIAN
GEORGE

THE SCARLET LIBRARY

FOREWORD

Writing in 1928, Émile Marcel, the editor of the fifteenth French edition of *Une Été à la Campagne* confidently proclaimed in his introductory note (reprinted in the present edition) that the author was a certain Gustave Droz. Had he still been alive, Droz, who died aged sixty-three in 1895, would no doubt have been both flattered and slightly amused.

He would have been flattered because, though he himself was not its author, *Une Été à la Campagne* had already established itself by the early years of the new century as something of a minor classic. This is clearly shown by the number of French editions of the work (and there have been a further half-a-dozen or so since 1928). Nor is the term 'minor classic' intended in any derogatory sense. In a country such as France, where the erotic is so well established as a genre that authors as acclaimed as Alfred de Musset, Théophile Gautier, Guy de Maupassant, and Paul Verlaine (among many others) have tried their hand at it, to produce a classic of any description is something of a feat. Moreover, given the witty and delicate style of *Une Été à la Campagne*, entirely free of the least trace of any vulgarity, such an attribution would tend to suggest that Droz's own work was of a comparable standard. This is

---

[1] Alexandrian, in his *Histoire de la littérature érotique* (1989), locates the novel – a masterpiece of 'malicious circumlocution' – in the 'pure tradition of French libertine literature' of the eighteenth century (p. 216).

possibly not far wide of the mark. His most popular novel, *Monsieur, Madame et Bébé* (1866), a collection of sometimes dangerously frank sketches about the intimacies and inconveniences of domestic existence, retains a certain charm more than a century later.

What might have appealed to Droz's sense of humour would have been the paradoxical thought that had he genuinely worked within the conventions of the erotic novel, rather than merely hovering about its fringes, some of his own works might still be read today. As matters stand, his reputation is in slow but inexorable decline. The 1959 *Oxford Companion to French Literature* still found room for a short entry about him; the editor of the 1995 edition did not extend the same courtesy. In fact, if Droz's name crops up at all today, it is as likely as not to be in connection with *Une Été à la Campagne* (1868) or another clandestine work falsely attributed to him, *Les Tableaux vivants* (1870).

If Droz's literary stock is on the wane, that of the real author of *Une Été à la Campagne* – Auguste Poulet-Malassis – is decidedly in the ascendant. This is due to a variety of reasons. First and foremost, of course, Poulet-Malassis is remembered as the publisher of Charles Baudelaire's *Les Fleurs du Mal* in 1857. In recent years, however, his subsequent career as editor, publisher, and, indeed, author of high quality erotic, licentious or pornographic works has been increasingly deemed worthy of interest in its own right. Thus, Claude

Pichois (Baudelaire's principal French biographer) published the first full length study devoted to the author of *Une Été à la Campagne* in 1996 (alas, still only available in French), a considerable amount of work of a bibliographical nature has now been published, and there is even a website hosted by an eminently respectable academic body devoted to his life and work.

Paul Emmanuel Auguste Poulet-Malassis was born in Alençon, a thriving town some 120 miles west of Paris, on 16 March, 1825. Although his family had been established there as printers since the sixteenth century, he himself, like many young men in the mid-nineteenth century, was irresistibly drawn to Paris. The French capital, however, especially during such a period of renewed political unrest, could be a dangerous place for a young man, especially one with printers' ink in his blood, advanced views on issues of personal morality, and a tendency towards fervent republicanism.

Hardly had he set foot in the capital before the Revolution of 1848 broke out. Poulet-Malassis, for his part, put the training he had received in the family business in Alençon to good use and immediately started up his own newspaper, an inflammatory rag called *L' Aimable Faubourien, journal de la canaille*. The venture did not survive for long: within a couple of weeks the editor was under lock and key, where he would remain for the next six months, being released just in time for Christmas at the end of the year.

Not surprisingly after this experience, Auguste Poulet-Malassis maintained something of a low profile for the next few years, returning to his studies (which was the reason that had brought him to Paris in the first place) and haunting the literary cafés and cheap eating houses. Indeed, it was at one of the latter, 'Chez la mère Perrin', that in the course of 1850 he met Baudelaire for the first time.

By 1853, Poulet-Malassis was back in Alençon, helping out at the family business along side his mother and his brother-in-law. It wasn't long though before he was ready to shake the dust of Alençon from his feet again. By the mid-1850s, following the death of his mother in 1855 (his father had died in 1850), he found himself in joint control of the family enterprise together with his brother-in-law, Eugène De Broise. Plans were soon afoot to establish a bookshop in Paris with a view to developing the publishing side of the business. In late December 1856, a contract was signed with Baudelaire for the first edition of *Les Fleurs du Mal*, and in January 1857 the shop opened in the rue de Buci.

From a commercial point of view, the publication of a volume of poetry by a virtually unknown author is not the ideal starting point for a venture of this kind. To make matters worse, Baudelaire proved an extremely difficult writer to work with, especially when it came to checking and authorising proofs. Neither Poulet-Malassis nor his brother-in-law could have foreseen, however, that within a few weeks of the book's appearance in June 1857, they would be embroiled in criminal proceedings for 'outrage à la morale publique'. Both the editors and the author were handed down a fine, and a number of the poems had to be removed.

Over the course of the next few years, Poulet-Malassis and De Broise would be no stranger to court proceedings. In 1858, the *Mémoires du Duc de Lauzun* earned them another fine and three months in prison; the following year they were in trouble again, this time over an edition of a book on Saint-Just. Nor were the problems they faced purely legal. Poulet-Malassis, despite (or because of) his literary flair, had an unreliable commercial sense coupled with a tendency towards bibliographical extravagence. As he himself wrote to the author Jules Champfleury, 'The main defect of my temperament is an indifference to money. The only thing I reproach myself about is that I have never been able to think of it as a tool. I lack the cardinal virtue of the epoch in which I live.'

In one year alone (1861) he managed to bring out more than seventy works, few of them likely to turn a profit. In the nick of time, his brother-in-law insisted that their partnership should be dissolved: De Broise retreated to the provincial safety of the family business in Alençon; Poulet-Malassis retained control of the Parisian side of operation.

Within a year, Poulet-Malassis was bankrupt. Between November 1862 and May 1863, he spent six miserable months being shunted around various debtors' prisons in Paris, sometimes being held in what was effectively solitary confinement.

The real question though was what was he going to do when he was finally liberated? It was time for a fresh start, somewhere with a more congenial regime, both politically and morally, than that to be found in France. Yet such a place would have to be predominantly francophone, would need to have an established book trade, and would need to be within easy reach of Paris. How else would he exercise his livelihood otherwise? Only one city fulfilled all these conditions: Brussels.

Poulet-Malassis had been harried from pillar to post by the authorities in Paris. Paradoxically, when one examines the catalogue of his publications (that for November 1861 runs to some thirty-six pages) during the late 1850s and early 1860s, one is mainly struck by the tremendous literary talent he had managed to assemble. Many of the writers he published may remain little known outside France (Charles Monselet, Jules Champfleury, or Charles Asselineau, for example), but their works are studied, and above all collected and read, there to this day. In Brussels, Poulet-Malassis would achieve something comparable but in a rather different domain.

Indeed, it might be said that, together with Jules Gay, he became one of the dominant publishers of French erotica throughout the 1860s. Thus, attention might be drawn to the *Parnasse Satyrique du Dix-neu-vième Siècle* (1864), a vast compendium of nineteenth century erotic poetry, or its companion volume, the *Nouveau Parnasse satyrique* (1866). One of his most original productions was *Le Théâtre érotique de la rue de la Santé* (1864; expanded 1866), a collection of short, extremely licentious plays which had been actually performed, though by marionettes, before a select audience of the authors and their friends. However, as Patrick Kearney remarks, collectors at the time would probably have particularly esteemed Poulet-Malassis's editions of authors such as Andréa de Nerciat, Béranger, and the Marquis de Sade: 'Between about 1866 and 1869, he published these and others like them in collaboration with a printer named Briard and a third man named Alphonse Lécrivain, and the fruits of this collaboration produced some of the most exquisite erotic books ever seen, recognizable at once by their fine printing, paper and design and their intelligent and scholarly Introductions and annotation.'(*A History of Erotic Literature*, 1982, p. 136.) The first edition of *Une Été à la Campagne*, with its elegant frontispiece by Félicien Rops showing Albertine and Adèle exchanging a kiss, is in this tradi-tion. (Rops, incidentally, was a great favourite of Poulet-Malassis, and did a considerable amount of work for him.)

Nonetheless, it wasn't all plain sailing during these years. Poulet-Malassis never really learned to appreciate Brussels or its inhabitants; a raid on the premises of Jules Gay, who acted as his Paris agent, resulted in a one year prison sentence being handed down to him *in absentia* in 1865; and he was plagued with ill-health. However, a general amnesty proclaimed in 1869 allowed him to spend his declining years in France where he died of consumption on 11 February, 1878. Despite being involved most of his life with the clandestine book trade, he had acquired a vast circle of friends and acquaintances, done as much to encourage new writing as almost any publisher in France (especially in the realm of poetry), and left an indelible mark on the history of erotic literature. *Une Été à la Campagne* is a fitting monument to a man whose real passion was for books.

– Terry Hale

THE ARTIST

Adrian George studied at the Royal College of Art in
the 1960s. He has had many one-man exhibitions of
his work and his images have been reproduced in
prints, postcards and posters all over the world. His
works are in the Victoria & Albert Museum, the
National Portrait Gallery and many private collections.
In the 1990s he lived in Paris and this city exerted a
subtle influence over the subject matter of his work:
his choice, therefore, to illustrate A *Summer in the
Country* is both appropriate and felicitous, as he is not
only francophile but also enjoys French literature of
the period. We are especiallly honoured as this is the
first time he has accepted a commission to illustrate so
specifically erotic a text.

SUMMER IN THE COUNTRY

The Correspondence of Two Young Parisian Girls
Edited by a Fashionable Author

AUTHOR'S FOREWORD

It will come as no surprise that the letters you are about to read, the work of two young ladies, were never intended for publication. How and under what circumstances they fell into my hands is of little import: what matters is only that the reader enjoys them for what they are.

Not having the slightest wish to pass them off as something they are not, however, I earnestly engage those whose minds are as narrow as their principles are austere (well, let us at least hope there is some correlation), those who are pious, chaste or prudish, in a word, all those who trust that their salvation can be purchased at the price of the mortification of the flesh and self-denial, to think carefully before opening this book; there can be no doubt that by so doing they will gravely compromise their chances of having a front row seat reserved for them when they get to Paradise.

On the other hand, I can recommend these letters

most warmly to those who ask of life only those things which are attractive and entertaining; to those gentlemen of mature years whose imagination is still ardent and vivid, but whose physical prowess, regrettably on the wane, should stand in need of some slight cordial; and I would especially commend these letters to the youth of both sexes who, though barely on the threshold of life, possess an entirely laudable ambition to instruct them-selves in the *ars amoris* and to harvest as efficiently as possible that store of pleasure which Mother Nature, in all her bounty, has seen fit to confer on them.

This said, and without further ado, let us call on our two charming scribes to speak for themselves.

Letter I: Adèle to Albertine

Paris.

Albertine B—[1]

Assistant Mistress,

Pensionnat V—,

—,

Nr Paris.

23rd April, 18—

My dearest Albertine,

You must think I have been ever so lazy or that I am purposely ignoring you, and it is most unfair of you! It isn't my fault if I haven't replied to your last letter, I want you to know I have been quite rushed off my feet.

---

[1] It is hardly necessary to remind the reader that dashes have been used to conceal the identity of the idividuals concerned, almost all of whom are still alive today.

Picture this: my uncle has been promoted to Colonel of a regiment in Algeria, and before taking up his new command he suddenly presented my aunt with a charming little cottage in the countryside where the merry widow is to remain until she comes out of mourning for her dearly departed overseas – about three months tops, I'd say. What's more, uncle has expressly instructed us to do lots of entertaining and to enjoy ourselves as much as we can. And all this has happened within the last month. I can leave you to guess how closely we intend to obey these instructions, the darling old fuddy-duddy!

This last fortnight I haven't had a minute to myself – what with dresses to buy, gowns to try on, all the attendant shopping for other things, not to mention having to accompany my aunt everywhere as she does her rounds. It's been a constant whirl of farewells and invitations to people to come and see us over the summer. Added to which there have been all the preparations for my uncle's departure to make. So you can see, my dearest Albertine, that I haven't had much time for putting pen to paper. But though I may not have been a very good correspondent, I have been thinking of you every day. How I miss you, when I'm all alone in my room, all alone in my bed; how I long for those nights we spent tenderly caressing each other! How often have I awoken from my sleep and looked for you by my side to beg a little service of you, a service that I have now been reduced to providing for myself!

And you, you wayward girl, do you still think of me

sometimes? I suppose you've got someone else on the go already... I warn you, if I find that's the case, I shall – well I shall go and snitch on you to the headmistress! I will tell her that her stern assistant school ma'm – who so ably instils a knowledge of the mysteries of ages past, the subtleties of French grammar, and the gems of literature in her charges – provides instruction in an entirely different subject – which comprises the greatest marvels to be found anywhere in the world – after nightfall!

In short, I have wept for you every night since I left the Pensionnat. I am only too aware that I need to leave all this behind me though, and I hope that my stay in the countryside will put me on the road to recovery.

We shall be off in two hours from now, but I didn't want to leave Paris without saying goodbye to you first. If you want to write to me, send your letter to B—, at Meulan.

Goodbye, my very special friend; I kiss your pretty red mouth a thousand times. Spare a thought for me now and then.

Your very own,

Adèle

Letter II: Albertine to Adèle

Paris.

27rd April, 18—

My darling Adèle,

You see how quickly I am replying to you! I suppose you must already be installed in your little place in the country by now, so I have sent this letter to B—, as you suggested. I am so glad that you think of me still, my little darling; I can promise you that you will be well rewarded! Two months apart already, and still no hope of us seeing each other! And me who wanted to spend the rest of my life with you!

Things have been much the same with me. We must learn to do without those delicious pleasures we shared together, which is by no means easy, or else learn to enjoy them on our own, which robs them of all their charm.

And what is all this business about snitching on me to the headmistress if you ever discovered I had allowed another to occupy that special place in my heart that I reserve for you! Let me tell you straight off that I am so in the headmistress's good books, and consequently those of her husband, that nothing you could possibly say about me would cause her to have the slightest doubt about my morals. They would roundly denounce you for telling lies and spreading untruths. Let me tell you, too, that since you left, all the older girls who stayed on, as well as all the new arrivals, are so ugly, so dull, so thin, so ungainly, or otherwise so offensive to the eye, that even if I were guilty of planning to replace you, I would have to give up the idea for want of a suitable partner.

Joking apart, my beautiful and adored little angel, I must admit that I have had to consider the possibility of seeking out a substitute for you. You know what my nature is like and how unprincipled I am: the former drives me on restlessly to satisfy my sexual desires at any price; the latter, or rather the lack of the latter, means that I would have felt no scruples or remorse in this regard; if I had only found someone capable of taking your place, I would have set about her conquest at once. But I can tell you, thanks to the spy-hole I have made which allows me to survey the entire dormitory at a glance, that even after secretly watching them for several nights in a row as they got ready for bed, its not so much a group of girls that I am called on to educate as a row of wooden planks.

The upshot of all this is that I have had no choice but to remain faithful to you, and to amuse myself, slender consolation though it may be, by thinking about you when I would much rather have held your lithesome young body in my arms.

Have you any idea how bored you will get, spending an entire summer so far from Paris? You who were so eager to learn everything there was to know, you who used to ask me questions that it was impossible to answer (for the very good reason that I hardly knew any more than you did since I have taught you everything I know!) Aren't you aware that the countryside is said to be the last resort of innocence, the very worst place you could imagine to find the answers to the questions that still puzzle you?

In any event, tell me everything you do and how you pass the time. Write to me as often as you like, it will give you something to do. For my part, I promise to let you know should I manage to find a replacement for you, however unsatisfactory.

Meanwhile, in exchange for the thousand kisses you kindly sent me in your last letter, I send back twice as many, half for your pretty little mouth, the other half for your adorable little breasts.

Your very own,

Albertine

Letter III: Adèle to Albertine

B—.

8th May, 18—

My dearest Albertine,

If you think I am bored here in the countryside, well all I can say is that you can think again! Not only am I not bored yet – which is hardly surprising since I only left Paris a fortnight ago – but I suspect that I shall enjoy myself here tremendously. This so-called 'last resort of innocence', as you term it, will in no small measure be responsible for me gorging on the fruit of the tree of knowledge, for which I have such a terrible hunger.

In the first place, I love the countryside, perhaps

because I have always been hemmed in by four walls until now; secondly, uncle's cottage – I won't refer to it pretentiously as 'my little place in the countryside' – is really very comfortable. What's more, it has one great advantage, an advantage you will readily appreciate, in that it houses a vast library which I can make use of at my discretion, or indiscretion even, judging by some of the works I've leafed through. For a great reader like myself, this is a real bonus. So every morning at about six – the weather here has been fabulous – just think of your little Adèle meandering along the paths in the garden, clutching a book, drinking in the fresh country air, and growing light-headed from reading poetry and the scent of the lilac trees! I never really experienced spring until I came to B—

Gentle and charming host,
unbidden by spinney or grove,
Bringing a blush to ripening fruit
and the budding rose.

You see! I must be learning something from all this reading, I'm already quoting lines of poetry.

After reading, there is music, which I also adore. My uncle has been kind enough to provide me with a piano in perfect working order. Then there is drawing and painting. There is an almost limitless number of enchanting views here that I have every intention of sketching. As you will admit, there is no reason whatsoever to be bored.

But this is not why I write. I told you in my last letter

that I would not fail to complete my education during my stay at B——. Well, I have discovered that the gardener, old V——, has two sons and daughters, while my aunt has brought with her from Paris a coachman, a footman, a chambermaid, and a cook – and, would you credit it, all these individuals are young, not at all bad looking, and, from what I have gathered, on the best of terms with each other.

There is a little wood at the bottom of the garden, and I fear that the murky depths of that place will prove fatal to any idea of rustic innocence. Nothing very much has happened so far, but it won't be long before matters take a more serious turn, and I intend to keep abreast of all the details.

Just imagine, everyone treats me as if I were a child, and makes not the slightest attempt to hide anything from me! I'm not far off eighteen, but you would think I was only fifteen from the way they behave – but, then, you know that shy air of childish innocence I can put on when I want to, so perhaps there's nothing to be surprised at. Didn't you yourself hesitate for quite a while before you showed your hand? And even then you were far from sure of me when you took the plunge!

So, as I say, it is just as if I wasn't there, the way everyone carries on, and you can be sure that I shall do nothing to awaken their suspicions.

There is one other factor in favour of my studies progressing well: the set of rooms I occupy couldn't be better situated. There are three rooms in all: a tiny boudoir, which is an absolute delight; a dressing-room;

and a closet, which I have turned into a studio, and where my piano is to be found. My aunt's bedroom is located on one side, while on the other there is the guest room, which is by far the nicest room in the house, and only ever occupied by close friends or important visitors who have to be entertained in style.

Still, I bet you are wondering, dearest Albertine, how this can possibly help me fill in the gaps in my education. Here is the answer: yesterday evening, while I was ferreting around in the studio, I discovered a chink in the wall, almost invisible to the naked eye, through which one can see everything that goes on in my aunt's room.

What luck had thrown in my way in the studio, I managed to copy with the same good fortune in my dressing-room with the result that there is a second spy-hole, no less discreet than the first, which makes me mistress of all the secrets of the guest bedroom. And, if that was not enough, both apertures are directly in line with the bed. Nothing can happen there without me having a ringside seat.

Now do you understand? My uncle doesn't intend to stay permanently in Algeria, but will return to B— from time to time; and it won't be for want of trying if the mysterious curtain which hides the secrets of his alcove isn't drawn back a fraction for my particular benefit. So much for the left hand side; as for the right, I have high hopes that it too may reveal the most succulent of secrets, which I shall certainly turn to my own advantage.

Added to that, the layout of my rooms is such that once the doors to my dressing-room and studio are closed, no-one can hear or see anything that goes on in my bedroom. Should circumstances dictate that, in the furtherance of my education, I might wish to progress from theory to practice, I can rest assured that my walls will have neither ears nor eyes to betray me. Not everybody is so fortunate.

In any event, I have oiled the locks on my doors; they are now discretion itself. I have practised opening and closing them, coming in and going out, such that the most attentive ear would not detect the least sound. When opportunity arises, it will not be my fault if anything goes awry. I have done everything that a good general can do to ensure victory.

Since we are each furnished with our own spy-hole, I am sure that we shall have much to tell each other that will lack neither variety nor curiosity value. My aunt is expecting a lot of visitors this summer, so watch out for some interesting stories. As for you, do try to find something else to observe other than your 'wooden planks', that really would be too depressing. The reason why I am writing to you today is that last night I dreamed of you. I leave you to guess what I did when I woke up!

If you guess correctly, return the compliment, dearest, while thinking of...

Your very own,

Adèle

Letter IV: Albertine to Adèle

Paris.

11th May, 18–

My darling little Adèle,

Without claiming to have the wisdom of the Sphinx, I've solved the riddle you set me in your last letter, and you can rest assured that I carried out your instructions to the letter.

I can hardly say how much I envy the good fortune which has plumped you down in the most perfect spot from which to observe all the goings-on at your uncle's cottage. If my reading of the future is to be trusted, you will soon be quite an expert in all these matters, and the knowledge you will acquire can hardly fail to rub off on me. Really, I blush to think that, though I am three years older than you, I have to depend on a mere stripling such as yourself for my education. It is not as if I have been desultory in my studies or shirked the hard work involved, the only thing that I have lacked is the opportunity, and that was out of my hands. After all, how much can one possibly learn in a girls' boarding school? Nothing, except for what we experienced for ourselves together! Admittedly, that was a step in the right direction, but just think of all the secrets which are still hidden from us!

Go on then, hurry up and become a world authority so that you can instruct me in turn. I look forward to your next letter with impatience. I shall have to finish mine sooner than I would have liked since the head-mistress has not been well and has asked me go and see her. Goodbye, my little darling! Remember that I am counting on you.

Albertine

Letter V: Adèle to Albertine

B—.

15th May, 18—

My dearest Albertine,

The whim took hold of me this evening to christen my spy-hole, the one on the left (in the studio), the room on the right being unoccupied at the moment. And, like Titus, I can honestly claim: 'I have not been wasting my time today.' In fact, I was able to watch my aunt getting ready for bed.

My aunt, if you remember, is a tall, beautiful woman of about twenty eight; her face is very attractive, and she has the most pretty teeth, which she takes good care to show off. Personally, I always imagined from her rather angular features, her slender fingers, and her long slim feet, that her crinoline must account for a considerable proportion of the area over which my uncle exercises sole rights of control between the hours of midnight and nine o'clock in the morning. I say 'sole rights' because I have the highest opinion of my aunt's uprightness of character. Well, my dear, I could not be more wrong and my uncle, who absolutely adores his wife, is a far more fortune man than I ever suspected. Really, his bed mate has a figure which would be the envy of a statue sculpted by Praxiteles or Pradier!

Of course, my aunt never suspected for one minute that my imprudent gaze was watching her every movement as she prepared for bed with the sort of freedom and abandon that only someone knowing they were completely unobserved could assume.

First, she unlaced her boots, revealing in the process a calf whose lovely shape would have done credit to Diana the Huntress. Then she took off her dress and I saw that her arms were fit to replace those missing from the Venus de Milo. Her corset soon followed her dress, and I found myself staring at breasts as firm as marble. I still hadn't recovered from my surprise when her petticoat slipped to the ground, allowing me to observe at my leisure her slender, supple waist, fully developed hips and thighs, and a bottom as round, and perfect, and exquisitely shaped as to make the Valléda in the Luxembourg turn crimson with envy, since she looks positively knock-kneed in comparison with my aunt!

As for the latter, she seemed to admire herself with the greatest pleasure in the wardrobe mirror which stands at the foot of the bed, and which obligingly reflected all these different and diverse charms so perfectly assembled in the body of a single woman. I suppose she was regretting that all these splendid features were of not the slightest use to her, given that my uncle was hundreds of miles away, busy chasing Arabs in the desert, when he might have cut such a dashing figure propped up in the feather-bed which would now harbour a lonely young woman with only her memories to keep her company.

I can tell you quite frankly that this bed aroused all kinds of longings in me. I would willingly have shared it, and I would have done my best to make the abandoned occupant forget the tedium of her temporary widowhood. I even wracked my brains to find some pretext with which to disturb my aunt, but the fear that my advances might be rejected restrained me. Believe me though when I admit to you that when my neighbour had got into bed and extinguished the light, I crept back to bed and began to do what I would willingly have done with a partner.

Dearest Albertine, you would have braved rejection, wouldn't you? And perhaps your audacity would have been crowned with glory. But as for me, I lack the courage.

Goodbye for the time being. I will write as soon as I have anything new. I send you a kiss as big as my love for you.

Adèle

Letter VI: Adèle to Albertine

B—.

16th May, 18—

My darling Albertine,

I bring you glad tidings! The very thing we have been waiting for has happened, and if that doesn't satisfy you, then nothing will.

Yesterday, in the course of the afternoon, my aunt received a letter from Africa which made her extremely happy. Uncle is well and he will not be away as long as we feared initially.

She went to bed early, and I followed shortly afterwards, not having any reason to stay up. I was quietly getting ready for bed when, as luck would have it, the idea seized hold of me of paying a visit to my spy-hole, which is just as well, or I would have missed one of the strangest sights you can ever imagine.

My aunt, dressed only in her camisole, was sitting in a chair directly facing me. She was bathed in a pool of light coming from a lamp on a little table and was busy re-reading the letter from her husband.

This letter must have contained some extremely affectionate remarks, since her face and expression became very flushed and lively. Suddenly, she closed her eyes and her head gently sank back against the chair rest. Her left hand, the one in which she held this passionate epistle, let it flutter to the table, while her right slowly slipped down until it caught hold of her night-dress which she pulled up almost unconsciously, lifting it high enough for me to make out her beautiful chestnut pubic fleece, whose graceful curls had been coquettishly trimmed. It immediately reminded me of someone else's pubic fleece, the identity of whom you may easily guess. After that, this hand deviously groped its way forwards, as if hesitatingly, moving inch by inch, with no apparent criminal intent, until it slid stealthily between her splendid thighs, which obediently parted to assist its passage. But then it suddenly got down to work and began to move rapidly up and down.

So far, nothing very unusual to report, you might be thinking. My aunt, dreaming of her absent husband, the husband whom she loves passionately, has been reduced to those methods which we poor girls call upon as often as possible to distract ourselves while we await some gentle knight errant who will only be too glad to spare us the pains of our labour.

Before you lose patience with me, here is the amazing part. My aunt, who seemed to be getting quite carried away, suddenly stopped short as if she had been struck by an idea. For a moment I thought she had guessed that she was being spied on, but this was a false alarm. She went over to the wardrobe and took out a pretty oblong box which she keeps locked in a drawer. She opened this box and took out a – well, I am not very sure what she took out: some strange sort of instrument, round and long, of a kind I have never seen before. She gazed lovingly at it for some moments before going back to the position I described a few moments earlier. Next, making an unobstructed route for it with her left hand, she held this peculiar object in the right hand and, despite fierce resistance, made it completely disappear in a place where it must have found itself trapped extremely tightly. At once some kind of struggle occurred. The intrusive article, as if suddenly aroused and taking full advantage of the situation in which it found itself, started to attack my aunt so ferociously that her gorgeous body began to squirm and shake in an absolute frenzy of movement until, completely over-whelmed, she collapsed. No doubt it was the shame of finding herself in such a predicament which caused her to moan and groan for some moments longer as she did.

After remaining motionless for a while in the armchair, in a pose that few painters ever have a chance of capturing from real life, my aunt, coming to her senses, liberated the serpent which she had had the imprudence to nurture in her bosom, carefully placed it on the bedside table, got into bed and blew out the candle.

I suspect that she did not go to sleep straight away for, still eavesdropping as I was, I heard some further heavy sighs, which I believe to have been caused by that eccentric choice of bed partner of hers in the absence of Colonel —. Not knowing what appellation to give the instrument in question, I decided that I would henceforth refer to it as 'Uncle'.

What do you think of that? Is not the name appropriate?

And what do you think of everything I witnessed last night? As for me, the effect of such a scene was that I didn't manage to sleep a wink all night, even when I did manage to drop off for a few moments, 'Uncle' always seemed to be the central focus of all my dreams.

Next morning, my aunt was as fresh as a daisy and looked as if she had had the best night's sleep in her life!

Goodbye, darling Albertine. Write soon and let me know what you think about all this.

With love,

Adèle

Letter VII: Albertine to Adèle

Paris.

19th May, 18—

My darling Adèle,

You ask me what I think of the contents of your last letter? But my dear little one, they make me think of so many things at once that I end up by hardly being able to think at all! The one certain fact is that I laughed until I cried at your description of your aunt's bedtime toy, and I think the name you have chosen for it is perfect. The other thing is that I would have given all the tea in China to have been able to witness such a performance. But while you get a free ringside seat, all I can do is deplore the tedium of my own life. In short, my pupils are just the same as always.

I can't get that devil of an 'Uncle' of yours out my head. Waking or asleep, he seems to hover before my eyes, like a ghost who you can never get rid of. And following on from your charming description of all your aunt's perfections, I can hardly bare to look at myself in the mirror. Try comparing yourself to a statue!

But I do agree with you about your aunt being a paragon of virtue. As young as she is, as lovely as she is, and as warm-blooded as she is – there can be no doubt about that in the light of what you've seen – to go and shut yourself off alone in the countryside, out of reach of the attentions of all your hosts of admirers, takes real courage.

Imagine! Instead of living in a world like a dream come true, she makes do with a grotesque parody of nature! Is that not truly an act of conjugal fidelity of heroic proportions?

And isn't your uncle – the real one, I mean – the luckiest man alive, a husband to be envied amongst husbands! I hope he at least appreciates the sacrifices which have been made on his behalf? Or is he just like all the others and thinks that this is quite natural and doesn't represent the least obstacle to him cheating on the woman who has taken such tremendous pains to keep herself pure and chaste for him! They are all the same, husbands! If ever I get married, I can promise you that the 'Uncle' I shall make use of when my husband isn't around won't be of the kind you can keep under lock and key!

I said just now that school goes on the same as always, neither better nor worse, which is true with regard to the pupils; but among the domestic staff, a new maid arrived a few days ago whom it might be worth taking some trouble over.

Without being exactly pretty, Félice has a very remarkable face. She is twenty four or twenty five years old, small, slender, and a brunette. She comes from Provence. Her hair is very beautiful, she has a slightly aquiline nose, and her eyes, which are grey-blue in colour, are round and large; in fact, they have a rather strange look about them, caused by the dark rings which surround them and her thick black eyebrows, which meet just above the nose. Her upper lip is lined with fine hairs, while a light down, compact and brownish in colour, runs down the side of her cheeks, not unlike the side whiskers of a first year student.

When I tell you that Félice has little white teeth, and dainty hands and feet, you will agree that she is not a girl who should be overlooked. So do not be astonished if I take a shine to her. In fact, I really do intend to give her a try, all that I have lacked so far is an excuse with which to commence hostilities, but I'm busily looking for one. I will keep you posted as to how I get on.

The indisposition of the headmistress, which I mentioned in my last letter, has grown worse and turned into something more serious. She has been in bed for more than a week now, and I have taken over as acting headmistress during that time (quite a promotion). In fact, I'm in sole command here which I don't mind in the least since I have always liked making myself obeyed, as you know.

The headmaster has shown every consideration towards me and has been most courteous.

Farewell. If you see anything else of note from your

eerie, don't fail to tell me: I would hate my education to suffer. As for me, remember my promises to you.

Love and kisses,

Albertine

Letter VIII: Adèle to Albertine

B—.

22nd May, 18—

My dearest Albertine,

Our solitude has been invaded: we have had a stream of visitors from Paris. You would hardly recognise B— any more, everything is so topsy-turvy.

First it was the turn of Maître J—, one of the most famous barristers in Paris, who won an important case for my uncle last year. He's very rich, or so they say. In appearance, he's a small man in his forties, somewhat solemn and preoccupied, who invariably wears a white tie. He has a deep voice, large eyes, a pimply complexion, and is in proud possession of six strands of hair which he combs forwards from the back of his neck over his head.

We've put him up in the guest-room. I must admit that this is rather an anti-climax as far as my right hand peephole is concerned, for I have no intention whatsoever of investigating what our pompous barrister does in the privacy of his chamber. And since he's here for the entire month, you will understand the adverse effect that his presence might have on my studies!

But we also have a young couple staying with us who were only married earlier this year. They are like a pair of turtle doves and I would very much have approved of them as my neighbours, at least I would have been sure of learning something. I did my best to arrange matters in their favour, but my aunt would have none of it: the barrister's greater status was undeniable, and with it went the best room.

We have also been honoured by the visit of a well known author and playwright. His plays are said to be very witty. I hope this is true – in any event they can hardly be less witty than his conversation. What a dull and tiresome individual!

And we are expecting more visitors yet! There is talk of a garden party, picnics, excursions in the countryside, and a boating trip. The Seine is almost next door to us. There has also been mention made of amateur theatricals. You cannot imagine how happy this makes me! I tell you, this summer will really be one to remember!

While waiting for all this to happen, we have organised some little recitals in the evening. The young bride is an excellent musician, while her husband always puts in a spirited performance, even if he's unlikely to win any medals for it.

This increase in our numbers has meant that we have had to take on more servants. One of the new recruits turned up at the door only this morning. I suspect that she represents a striking contrast to the Félice on whom you wish to slake your evil designs. Here is her description.

She comes from Normandy, and she is blonde, barely

eighteen years old, and is even taller than my aunt (who, you will remember, is by no means short for a woman herself). But how perfectly proportioned she is with it! She is all curves, a complete superabundance of flesh!

And that's not all: just imagine that this formidable body is surmounted by a round, cherubic little face, with perfectly clear eyes and an almost childlike expression. In short, she's got a real *baby face*!

You ought to see the lust in their eyes when the men – masters and servants alike – turn their gaze on her.

Even Maître J— has quite cast off his inexorable gravity. At the sight of our young Normandy lass's dazzling freshness and sumptuous charms, his great eyes opened wide and glowed as bright as burning embers, the colour of his nose deepened from red to crimson, and his six strands of hair positively bristled.

I have no idea what will come of all this, but I fear for Mademoiselle Rose's virtue. It will certainly be subject to some outrageous liberties. As from this moment, I shall not let her out of my sight, and I have no doubt that I shall have some more news for you before very long.

As for you, my dearest Albertine, I wish you every success in the siege you are about to undertake. Above all, keep me informed of how you get on.

Your own,

Adèle

Letter IX: Albertine to Adèle

Paris.

26th May, 18—

My darling little Adèle,

The siege here has been of rather shorter duration than that at Troy. I am mistress of the situation, and the position which you left vacant three months ago has now been filled.

And now you'd like the details, I expect.

This is how I arranged my artillery. Yesterday morning, when I went to visit the headmistress, whose condition is worsening daily, I complained of a slight indisposition. By lunch time the pain had become much worse without, as you might imagine, me being able to offer any precise indications as to the nature of the problem: sometimes it was a headache, sometimes it was nerves. Oh, yes, the nerves – especially the nerves!

That evening I was due to sit up with the headmistress, as I do every night, but I soon felt so unwell that her husband had to insist that I took myself off to bed, offering to keep his wife company himself, and instructing Félice, whose room is quite close to mine, to keep a watchful eye on me.

This was exactly what I had been planning. I got up with a little sigh and made my way, a trifle groggily, towards my bedroom, with my favourite chambermaid in tow.

By the time I got there I was so prostrate that I had to be helped to undress. After I'd had a cup of camomile tea in bed, I was feeling much better though, and I sent

Félice off to tell my employer's husband that he was not to worry on my account, since I had recovered from my indisposition and all I needed was a good night's rest.

Once I was satisfied that everything was safe from this direction and the messenger had returned safely, I suffered another attack. Having been rather a vague sort of ailment until this moment, my indisposition now made up its mind that it was a nervous problem, and I waved my arms about and writhed around in my bed as appropriate. Félice, completely bewildered by this stage, had just suggested that she should fetch the head-mistress's husband when, amazingly enough, the attack suddenly came to an end. As a result, she decided to spend the night with me, and drew up a chair by the side of the bed.

After an uneventful quarter of an hour, I suggested that she should go back to her own room. Naturally, she declined. The upshot of this was that, to salve her conscience, I told her that I would allow her to share my bed with me; that way, if a fresh attack came on, she would be there to help me.

After some humming and hawing, she made up her mind to accept this proposition.

The critical moment was at hand.

There was my Félice taking off her dress, petticoat, and corset, while I watched everything out the corner of my eye; as she removed her garments one by one, I discovered just how gracious and pure was her body, though still that of an adolescent.

Finally, she got into bed!

Once I felt her next to me, my whole body was gripped by a kind of fever. In consequence of having pretended to be sick, I had almost become ill in earnest. The strength of my desire for her – for the last week I had observed the strictest continence in expectation of this happy moment – and the fear of rejection, not to mention my apprehensions of the scandal which might result, combined to produce such a shock to my nervous system that my teeth began to chatter and I was wracked by a trembling fit that I was powerless to control.

In fact, my darling Adèle, it could be said that I played my role to perfection.

First, I asked Félice to put out the candle because, I said, the light prevented me from sleeping.

After this precaution had been effected, and I had allowed five minutes to pass by (five centuries more like!), and unable to restrain myself any longer, I turned towards her, with a deep sigh. She asked me whether I was suffering.

'Terribly, my dear,' I replied.

Then, suddenly pouncing on her, I threw my arms around her neck, as if begging for help, and hugged her to me.

This advance did not meet with the hostile reception I had anticipated; on the contrary, I thought that I detected a slight pressure in response to my own. The young girl would have done anything to relieve my suffering!

Encouraged by this opening move, and my appetite further whetted by an early success, I pinioned her tightly in my arms, still groaning and complaining about the wretched state of my nerves. Then, with a cautious hand, for I had no wish to alarm her, I began to explore her body, which I soon discovered was as fresh, supple and enticing as I had imagined and that her skin was delicate and soft.

Encountering no resistance, and feeling that I was being encouraged rather than repulsed, I decided to attempt a major advance. I slipped my left arm around Félice, pressed my lips against hers while, forcing her knees apart, I slid my right hand gently between her velvety thighs which, far from trying to arrest my progress, seemed positively to anticipate my every move.

By now I was almost at my goal – almost! Suddenly, I pulled back my hand and let out an exclamation of surprise to which my Provençal girl reacted with a long peal of hysterical laughter.

I can imagine your amazement at this moment! You must be wondering what on earth could have stopped me in my tracks like that, especially such pretty tracks as these? Why the laughter? Why my dismay? In your last letter you mention a certain pubic fleece, well known to both of us, 'whose graceful curls had been coquettishly trimmed...' Well, my dear girl, if what you referred to could be called a fleece, what might you possibly call what I had just felt? At the very least I must have stumbled on a forest, perhaps not as virgin as those to be found in the Americas, but almost as impenetrable. Or rather – no, let's not go groping after unlikely metaphors. Very well, call it a fleece if you will, a veritable fleece: bushy, bristling, tangled, rough and unkempt to the touch. It was more like a goatskin of the kind Jacob covered himself with to trick good old Isaac, which made me think, incidentally, that the tribe of Esau is by no means extinct. There could be no doubt about it: Félice must descend directly from the line of the hairy patriarch who was so partial to lentils.

But to get back to my story.

When Félice's laughter had died down, and I had recovered from my shock, the wicked girl confessed to me that for the last quarter of an hour or more she had guessed what I was up to and had not been in the least taken in by my attack of nerves. Nonetheless, she had let me play my hand right to the end, being curious to know what effect it would have on me when I put my hand on the strange shock of hair which adorns her body. The result had been worth waiting for.

Thinking back over the yelp I had so naturally let out and the abrupt way I had withdrawn my hand, we both began to laugh uncontrollably, and the closest and most good-humoured friendship was established between us as a result. Félice took hold of my hand, which was still rather hesitant, and took me on a conducted tour of those dense thickets that I could still only penetrate after some effort. She soon proved to me by her transports of delight – as intense as they were often repeated, that she was no less devoted than I am to those pleasures which had involved me in so much unnecessary diplomatic activity.

In short, we were extremely pleased with each other and we spent the rest of the night in gainful employment. When, the next morning, the headmistress and her husband enquired whether I had recovered from my indisposition, they concluded from the dark rings under my eyes and from the tired look on my face that I must have slept badly, and they extended their sympathy to me.

Well, I've kept my word, as you can see. That's the story of my latest conquest down to the last detail. Now it's your turn.

Devil take that wretched little lawyer of yours! What business was it of his to turn up like that and ruin a perfectly good lesson in Natural History which could have proved so instructive? And right from the start, too! Fortunately, the resources offered by B— are more than a match for the likes of him.

Goodbye for the present, my darling Adèle. I send you my hugs and kisses. Remember I shall always love you, despite my flagrant infidelity.

Your very own,

Albertine

Letter X: Adèle to Albertine

B—.

28th May, 18—

My dearest Albertine,

My congratulations! What a courageous Amazon you are! You truly deserve your laurels. Though all your prudence and deviousness proved unnecessary in the event, a wise general never goes into battle without having made some provision for a possible retreat. I praise and admire you with regards to the strategy you felt it incumbent to adopt.

You ought to know, however, that the portrait you have painted for me of your hirsute antagonist is rather frightening. I can quite understand your hesitation, almost to the point of you turning tail, and I am sure you needed all the courage with which your are endowed in order to triumph over this monster. Fancy finding like that, in the dead of night, at the moment you'd least expect it, a wild beast right under your hands.

You said in your last letter but one that you can't get the thought of 'Uncle' out of your head. Now I find I am in the same situation, only I am haunted by a vision of the spine-curdling creature that you described to me.

Which makes us quits. I will swap my 'Uncle' for your she-bear. Is it a deal?

I suspect that you are quite right with regards to Félice's ancestry, and in accordance with my passion for giving people nicknames I shall call her, with your permission, 'Mademoiselle Esau', which would seem to suit her down to the ground.

And now to return to B—, not that there is anything new to report, but plenty of things are in the offing, and at the moment, contrary to what the collective wisdom of mankind teaches us, I am chasing after an assortment of hares at the same time.

Let's start with Mademoiselle Rose, about whom all the men are hovering like bees round a honeypot: our monotonous playwright, our newly married husband (that's men for you!), and our little lawyer.

None of these gentlemen has the slightest suspicion that I am constantly spying on them and that they cannot even lift their little finger without me knowing about it. The first two are getting nowhere fast: X— is the dullest man alive, and the other is under the thumb of his wife.

But as for the lawyer, he has commenced the siege in regulation fashion, and he presses on with the job in hand with an energy of which I would not have imagined him capable.

I wouldn't be at all surprised if he doesn't come in ahead of the field.

But the servants haven't been left standing either. The coachman, who is a handsome lad (trust me), has been limbering up to some purpose and is now completely neglecting his little Victoire, the youngest daughter of V—.

It's been a few days now since I saw him making his way, about nine o'clock of an evening, to the edge of the little copse at the bottom of the garden while the simple-minded gardener's daughter, thinking no-one will put two and two together, trots off in the direction of the other side of the woods. It's obvious that Victoire-Ariane is most put out.

As for Rose, she doesn't need to move an inch. There is a veritable steeple-chase in progress, and she is the steeple. So far, she hasn't seemed to take much interest, but I'll keep my eye on her anyway. What makes this so easy to achieve, especially at night, is the fact that she sleeps in a tiny room at the end of the same corridor where the lawyer, my aunt and I have our apartments.

You would not believe how busy I have been, my dearest Albertine. I don't know when I find time to sleep. And you who thought I would have succumbed to a fatal dose of boredom long ago!

And that's not all. I have to keep a watch over the barn which Madame Pruneau (as in 'prune'– but don't look at me, that really is her name), our cook (and very good she is too), is in the habit of visiting.

To understand the significance of this you need to know that the farm buildings are under the day to day management of M. Nicholas, Mademoiselle Victoire's younger brother, a very polite fair-haired boy whose education has been taken in hand by our Madame Pruneau, a buxom, rosy-cheeked farmer's wife, thirty years old if a day.

The worthy Monsieur Pruneau is a chef somewhere in England at the moment, so it's only fair that his wife should find something to keep her amused closer to home. Her job as a cook here takes up most of the day, but it leaves the evenings free for her to pursue her education.

I am hoping to be able to catch one of her lessons

before too long. It shouldn't present too many difficulties to hide myself behind some innocent looking bale of hay. Most of these lessons happen between ten and eleven o'clock at night. How the desire for knowledge overcomes every obstacle that is put in its way!

I am collecting material for my next letter.

Goodbye for the present, dearest Albertine. I send you my kisses, but you had better not mention them to Madame Esau – she might be jealous.

Your very own,

Adèle

PS An elderly female cousin arrived yesterday (which is not very interesting) together with a very pleasant young man called Monsieur Lucien P— (which is more to the point). We have already been introduced, and he twice asked me to dance with him last Christmas, at the only ball I've ever been to. We have now renewed our acquaintance. He really is very agreeable and has shown himself most kind and attentive. One's never too sure of these things, but – well, who knows?

Goodbye again.

Letter XI: Albertine to Adèle

Paris.

1st June, 18—

My darling Adèle,

Your last letter concluded with an enigmatic 'but', which sent my mind racing. What a little word it is, and how much more it says than you would guess from its length.

Could it be that Mademoiselle's heart has mumbled its first words? Could it be that Monsieur Lucien, who sounds as if he has been invested with all the powers of Cupid, is the mortal destined to pick that exquisite rose which I have been allowed to touch but not to gather?

I shall expect a detailed account of everything that happens. In view of all the lavish details you supply me with concerning other people, I do hope you do not intend to be economical about matters relating to yourself.

I have certainly set you a fine example, at any rate, and I shall now add some further remarks about your successor, Mademoiselle Esau, as you call her.

What a teacher that girl is, and what rapid progress I've made under her tuition!

The subject of our never-ending discussions at night, the thing which used to seem so mysterious and inexplicable to us, now appears as plain and clear to me as if I could see it with my own eyes. Apart from some practical experience, I am as well informed as the most brazen adventuress – and all thanks to Félice's tutelage.

I should say at once that she has the most remarkable

energy. She has pursued her studies to the very limit and can rightly boast of being an expert in all the arts. What *hasn't* she done! And, more to the point, what have other people not been allowed to do to her!

I can only laugh at myself when I think of my feigned illness. Nobody ever took such unnecessary precautions with such comic seriousness.

You can't even imagine, my darling Adèle, how much fun I am having at night – though I would have to admit that your evenings sound more charming. Still, they are so utterly different that it would be odious to make comparisons.

Félice is insatiable. You hardly get a moment's peace when she's around. The nights are not long enough for her, so she makes the most of any chances that occur during the day as well, and if those chances don't materialise quickly enough, then she will manufacture them out of thin air. What you and I used to do together, my darling, was nothing more than kindergarten stuff. All quite innocent! We did no more than learn our alphabet, take the first tottering steps together in our education. How amazed you would be if I could demonstrate everything I have learned to you today!

There is one thing above all, a thing we never even dreamed of, which is more delightful than anything else; and, once you know it, it seems the most natural thing in the world.

Let me do my best to explain it, relying on your incredible powers of intuition to fill in anything which my description may leave unclear.

To tell the truth, I wouldn't make such a mystery of it if we were lying next to each other in bed, and you would understand everything I say, I am quite sure, without having to tax your imagination to the full.

Old Aesop got it right, my dear, when he said that the tongue is the best thing there is in the world, though among the various purposes which he assigned to it, he didn't manage to mention the one that my highly experienced teacher has revealed to me.

What a source of indescribable pleasures is this organ of speech, and how well Esau's female descendant has learned to use it. You feel as if you are dying of pleasure!

Oh, my little darling, what debts of pleasure we owe each other! We should settle our accounts as soon as possible. You must learn to accept pleasure with a willing reciprocity and to return that same pleasure to your partner: do unto others as you would have them do unto you! Above all, never flinch before what Molière has called the instrument of man's omnipotence.

Now, if I have managed to give you a clear enough idea of the nature of Félice's virile prerogative, and it must be admitted that nature has bizarrely over-endowed the girl in this respect, you will understand how arduous the ordeal has been which I have had to undergo. What obstacles to overcome, what difficulties to surmount! Fortunately, as you said, courage is the one thing I don't lack; after rapidly surveying the size of the task ahead of me, I threw myself into it head first, and I came out of my trials with my honour intact.

Good God! It's just something you have to get used to!

You'll soon learn to do it, I promise you, and you'll eventually end up by enjoying doing it!

Félice is very pleased with me; she claims that before long I will be as good at it as she is. I call this plain flattery.

To change the subject slightly, I mentioned that 'Uncle' of yours to her. She explained everything about it to me and how one uses it. She also told me the proper name for this tool employed in the consolation of lonely girls. The word, with its bizarre spelling, is so peculiar that my pen refuses to write it down. It is another one of those things which one might talk about in whispers, but which it is better not to put down on paper.

Enough of such matters. I have some sad news to tell you: the headmistress is seriously ill. The doctors have been called in and have consulted among themselves; her husband knows not which way to turn.

Write soon, my darling Adèle.

Albertine

Letter XII: Adèle to Albertine

B—.

5th June 18—

My dearest Albertine,

I understand perfectly, my dear, everything is crystal clear. My powerful intuitions, as you so flatteringly say, followed you step by step, without taking a single wrong turn, through the dark labyrinth from which you fortunately managed to emerge unscathed. The main reason, I admit, why it was so easy for me to do this is because the thought of making a little 'excursion into the forest' with you had occurred to me more than once, and I can only wonder why we never got round to it. If you had suggested it to me, I would readily have accepted, even if I would never have dared propose such a thing myself. Sometimes one has the most peculiar reticences! If only we could have that time all over again!

But it seems as if the experienced Mademoiselle Esau is helping you make up for lost time in the most agreeable way possible. I know how carefully you laid your plans, but I can only congratulate you on having found such a treasure. The girl is a marvel, and I would be fascinated to see just how expansive this impressive symbol of her virility really is.

Since I am denied such a vision, I pass on to a subject which is more interesting, from my point of view that is.

You guessed right first time, my dear. Yes, I am the flame of his life, and he is the flame of mine – though I have buried this secret deeply in my bosom lest my eyes betray me. One should never throw oneself at people.

If only you knew how seductive my Lucien is! I shall sketch you his portrait, that way you can tell me what good taste I have. Don't worry, I shall be quite impartial, though my detachment won't go so far as to do him any injustice. After all, it's not my fault if he really is divinely charming, is it? There's nothing I can do about it.

Let me begin with his appearance. He's twenty seven years old, of medium build, and his face is lively and attractive. He's got large, blue eyes, which are so expressive that they can communicate all manner of feelings, thick brown hair, he doesn't wear any side whiskers, but he possesses a fine black moustache which frames teeth that are as white as pearl.

So what do you think? Does he take your fancy? Could you be any more amazed if I further told you that Lucien has the hands of an aristocrat, slender feet, that he is an excellent gymnast, that although always impeccably groomed, his clothes are simplicity itself, and that he is a skilled equestrian? Nor is this just my opinion, all the women here think the same way and, although you might never have guessed it, the men as well.

So, on the first point, there is complete agreement.

What about his character though?

Much as I may be loathe to do so, I have to admit that his intellectual qualities are the equal of his exterior perfections in every way.

I know you'll say I am exaggerating and try to pull the wool from my eyes, even dismiss Lucien as a character out of a novel. But what more can I do? I cannot deny the evidence or attempt to disguise the truth.

If everybody finds him pleasant, good humoured, and witty, I have no choice but to join in the general chorus of approval. I see though that I am forced by the exceptional nature of the circumstances to provide you with one or two further points for you to be able to appreciate him properly.

There is not the slightest trace of fatuousness about him, and he never seeks to draw attention to himself. Yet, when he does speak, he is perfectly at ease with everybody; in fact, whenever he does talk, people in other groups crane their necks to hear what he is saying. Although he can be tremendously sarcastic when he chooses, his choice of words is always extremely elevated, and he prefers to take the world as he finds it.

The one thing he can't abide is people who are self-important, as X— finds out to his cost every day. He speaks several languages, he sketches and paints, reads aloud well (his voice is perfectly modulated), is a good accompanist, and I have seen some delightful verse penned by him.

There you are then! A true to life portrait of my Lucien. (What an enchanting name, by the way. I repeat it to myself all day long!) Absolutely true to life, Mademoiselle, whatever you may think or say.

Dearest Albertine, do you really think it would be possible to resist such a man as this, a man who lets no occasion go by without showing you that he is by no means indifferent to you, or paying you some pretty compliment or pressing your hand, and who looks at you with eyes that make you want to melt? Personally, I

declare that resistance is impossible, and I throw myself on his mercy.

Do you remember my description of my little set of apartments? They possess, if you remember, the double advantage of being impeccably situated for spying on everybody else at the same time as being immune to prying eyes looking in from the outside. After having enjoyed the first of these benefits, I thought it high time to make use of the second. A theoretical knowledge of my subject is not sufficient for me, you see; I am determined to embark on my practical training. The hour has struck, the pupil is restive, eager to please, and (vanity apart) shows tremendous promise and willing. With such a perfect teacher as this, her education is bound to make great strides, if only he would consent to come and give her some private tuition.

There is more and more talk at B— about amateur theatricals. X— (it really is the first time he has shown himself to be the slightest bit useful) has rustled up a little one act comedy in which I have a role and Lucien too. We play the part of two lovers, of course. But matters seem to be coming to a head here. By the end of June or the first week of July – a month of holding him at arm's length seems to me more than anyone could reasonably expect – you should steel yourself to hear the complete and uncensored confession of Adèle. I have never kept anything back from you, and I won't now.

Quite apart from this, I need to be thinking of pressing on with my studies generally, which are in something of a trough at the moment. Nothing much is happening in my aunt's room – could 'Uncle' have fallen from grace? Perhaps he only puts in a ceremonial appearance on days when a letter arrives from Algeria? But we have not received a word for a month. Rose seems unassailable. I would have put money on Madame Prune, but there is still no news on this front. I have found a way of getting into the barn though, the only trouble is getting out again. I have no intention of finding myself trapped like a mouse.

So, all in all, everything is at a standstill.

I end my letter by repeating after you: enough of such matters. I hope your next letter will bring me better news of our poor headmistress, she is such a kind woman, and she has been so good to us.

I look forward to your next letter.

Your own,

Adèle

Letter XIII: Albertine to Adèle

Paris.

7th June, 18—

Dear Adèle,

Alas, I bring you not the glad tidings for which you were hoping but the worst imaginable news. Our dearly beloved headmistress died last night at three o'clock in the morning. She will be greatly missed by all who knew her, etc., etc., etc.

[A long panegyric ensues which is little more than a paraphrase of the famous discourse with its well turned phrase: *Madame se meurt, Madame est morte!* (My lady is dying, my lady is dead.)

It seemed unnecessary to preserve for posterity Mademoiselle Albertine's ponderous foray into similar territory.

For those readers for whom such allocutions are not without a certain lugubrious appeal, their attention is drawn to the Abbé Bossuet's funeral oration on behalf of Henrietta of England in 1670. The effect is largely the same whichever text one chooses to read.]

Letter XIV: Adèle to Albertine

B—.

9th June, 18—

Dear Albertine,

The headmistress is dead! Even now, I can hardly believe it. How terrible it is to die so young, so full of life, etc., etc., etc.

[At this point we suggest that the reader might like to turn to Malherbe's *Consolation* addressed to Du Perrier:

As a rose she has lived, as the roses do live

Not that we would possibly wish to infer by this that Mademoiselle Adèle is a jot less eloquent than Mademoiselle Albertine, or even the Eagle of Meaux.

The assistant mistress has indeed produced a pupil who is a credit to her in every regard.]

Letter XV: Albertine to Adèle

Paris.

20th June, 18—

My darling Adèle,

What I am about to tell you will seem incredible, yet I swear it is the gospel truth. This is not something that I could mention lightly, and I wanted there to be no possible room for doubt, to be completely sure of my facts, before writing to tell you what I have suspected for some time. The headmistress's husband, who on the day of the funeral, was so overwhelmed with grief that he could hardly bare to be separated from his wife's body, who talked insensibly of being buried alongside her in the grave, has already found a means of consolation. Indeed, he has found the most radical means of consolation imaginable. A fortnight is all it has taken for his tears, tears which he promised would spring eternal, to dry themselves completely.

Yet I can assure you that this is the case, and you'll believe me all the more when I tell you that it is from me that he seeks and hopes to procure that consolation.

It started – quite innocently, I'd like to imagine – with us crying on each other's shoulders. But for the last couple of days I have started to notice that his grief looks suspiciously like affection. Then, yesterday, it was the turn of the long glances, the languishing sighs, the little hugs, and the casual placing of his hand on parts of my body which are better left untouched, all of which told me that it would not be long before the dam burst.

As soon as I got an inkling of this, the strangest idea flashed through my brain, an idea which will take some courage to put into practice. But what if I were to take the place of the headmistress? In fact, this is exactly what I intend to do.

Of course, he's getting on for forty. But apart from the fact that his hair is thinning slightly, which is not the end of the world anyway, he really is in excellent shape. He has money of his own, and the school brings in a tidy bit as well, so it would be quite a good match for me, especially since I do not have a penny to my name. Thus, I would be lady and mistress of the house – which really has been my dream all along.

If I am going to carry this through successfully, the first thing is that I must never step down from this lofty pedestal of virtue which I've somehow managed to clamber upon.

Consequently, I have had to proceed with circumspection. Without saying a word, I lifted up the hand which was causing the problem and returned it to its proprietor. Then, surveying him as icily as possible, I rose to my feet in the most majestic manner imaginable – just like an insulted empress – and slowly swept out the room. After that, I shut myself in my bedroom, leaving him speechless and confused in my wake. He still hadn't found his tongue when I came down for breakfast next morning. I have him in the palm of my hand!

Enough of such serious matters, my dear Adèle, what about you? I am sure that your Lucien is everything you say he is, and nor do you, charming creature that you are, deserve any less. So what is new? Please write to me soon.

And what about Mademoiselle Rose, I'm interested in her, too – has she capitulated yet?

And Madame Prune? I haven't forgotten her either.

Come on, put pen to paper quickly! It's been two weeks since I received any news from you. But above all, please try to make something happen.

Between ourselves, I am beginning to get extremely fed up of Félice and I am looking for a way of getting rid of her which will not give rise to recriminations.

Goodbye for now, my darling Adèle, I send you my hugs and kisses. Make your next letter an especially long one.

Albertine

Letter XVI: Adèle to Albertine

B—.

23rd June, 18—

My dearest Albertine,

Your humble and obedient pupil, Ma'am, prostrates herself before your sovereign will. You demand a long letter: I shall perform miracles, if that is what is required, in order to oblige you.

Satisfied? If I already address you with all the respect

due to the governess of a renowned seat of learning, it is because I have not the slightest doubt as to the success of your plan. How could the gentleman in question possibly resist such grace, beauty and, above all, virtue rolled into one?

Speaking of virtue, I would love to have been there when you made your exit. Oh, Albertine, you must have been magnificent, and I can imagine from here the look of consternation on the poor widower's face as the consolation he so desired was whisked away from under his nose. I do hope he gets over it without making too much of a song and dance. My intuition tells me that in a few month's time you will not be in a position to refuse him anything.

But since the good gentleman has put such a brave face on the loss of his wife, and in such a short time too, I don't see why we shouldn't do likewise.

We must stop talking about our bereavement. This is not the right moment.

In fact, there are a lot of things happening here. During the interruption in our correspondence, I've collected masses of information about everyone, which I will now share with you.

First of all, I have found a way of observing Madame Pruneau's antics without running the slightest risk of finding myself a hostage to fortune amidst the bales of hay. It was a tricky problem, and this is the solution I found for it.

The barn is lit by two large dormer windows. One of these, which is set about ten feet off the ground, opens on to a large shed in which all manner of gardening implements are stored higgledy-piggledy. Among these I noticed a ladder leaning against the wall.

It was as if a shaft of light had struck my mind. Now I had the means, all I needed to do was to watch out for the opportunity to present itself.

For four days, I waited in vain. But one evening, around eleven o'clock, as I was standing guard behind my curtain, I heard young Nicholas cough as he walked in front of the kitchen. Then I saw him disappear in the direction of the barn.

A few moments later, the bulky form of Madame Pruneau, dressed in the scantiest attire, emerged from the kitchen door. After peering around, and seeing nothing to cause her alarm, she set off in the same direction with the skittish gait – her steps being as large as they are long – of a hippopotamus.

Without wasting a second, I nipped down the stairs and gained the barn in my turn, but from the opposite direction.

The ladder was propped against the wall just beneath the window. I quickly scaled the ladder, and soon I could look down right into the barn.

Unfortunately, the moon only peeped through the cloud cover from time to time, so that although I could hear everything perfectly clearly, I only caught the most fleeting glimpses of what was going on.

At the moment I took my seat in the box, the conversation was quite animated. I won't even try to replicate it. Madame Pruneau, who was holding forth, does not always choose her words in accordance with perfect good taste, but that evening she made use of a host of technical terms which completely baffled me, and which I am fairly certain are not to be found in Bescherelle or the Dictionary of the Academy.

The main issue to emerge from these discussions was that she had been, like Penelope, separated from her husband for an entire year; and prudent housewife that she was, she had no intention of presenting her good Ulysses, on his return to the conjugal Ithaca, with one or two contraband Pruneaux that she could not reasonably foist off on him as his own offspring. This debate went on for some time. Young Nicholas, carried away on a tide of adolescent passion, could not bring himself to comply with the sound advice proffered by his more knowledgeable instructress with regards to the infallible means of preventing disagreeable consequences.

The impetuous student finally caved in before the overwhelming arguments of the wise matron. He calmed down, their words grew less acrimonious, became disjointed, finally petered out... Alas, I could distinguish no more than a black shape moving frantically in the depths of the shadows.

I was in despair of gleaning the least bit of new information from this lesson conducted in the dark when a faint moonbeam pierced the clouds, allowing me to distinguish Nicholas, who had evidently trusted to fate, lying stretched out on his back with his face to the sky, while the hulking cook straddled his torso, facing the other way, her face transfixed on the ground, apparently in the midst of some bizarre ceremony performed on the body of her victim in the course of which she showed the most commendable zeal.

The ray of light faded, but not before I had seen Nicholas, trembling like an epileptic, frantically grab hold of the head of his tormentor, who brought her activities to a conclusion before endeavouring to calm him down by smothering him in kisses and caresses.

A short silence followed this performance. This was broken by Madame Pruneau, who congratulated herself on her rare foresight and sought to prove to Nicholas, on the strength of the present evidence, that had he not followed her precepts, he would almost indubitably have found himself the author of some hypothetical Pruneaux in the not too far distant future.

Once this lesson had clearly been assimilated, the fount of knowledge set to work imparting another. This time I noted that although she maintained the same position astride her fair-haired swain, she had turned round. In this way she almost buried the lad's head under her own voluminous person. Now she looked more like some bizarre kind of bare-back rider as she galloped along hell for leather until, seized by a similar nervous spasm (perhaps it is contagious), she suddenly capsized on top of him, uttering the most fearful sighs as she did so, which might easily have been mistaken for the lowing of cattle!

My curiosity was no longer as keen as it had been by the time this second lesson was concluded and I felt dreadfully tired. I clambered down the ladder and went back to bed, trying to figure out what exactly I had seen and heard. But before I had managed to do that, I had fallen asleep.

The reason I am telling you all this is so that you can ask Mademoiselle Esau about it: I have the utmost confidence as to her experience of such matters.

The lovely Rose, in whom you also expressed interest, should soon decide on her partner, unless I am very much mistaken. The negotiations have been moving on at a furious pace and, as I predicted, it looks as if it is the lawyer who will prove master of the field. Certainly he has taken over the reigns, and the odds must favour him. The young bridegroom has been handicapped by the presence of his wife, and X—, the playwright, by his fatuousness. Both were left standing at the start. Charles, the coachman, had an outside chance, but has made a hash of it. He went off like a bolt of lightning, with the result that Rose took fright. Though not so showy, the little lawyer has good staying power as he approaches the finishing line. A few more days, and I will announce the result.

You also ask at what stage I am at with Lucien. I am at the stage, my dearest Albertine, at which I find him more and more adorable, and every day I am more in love with him. If only you knew how my heart skips a beat, how it literally oozes with happiness, when our hands touch, when he puts his arm round my waist, when his mouth brushes against my cheek or my hair!

For his part, he has not the least idea, the poor boy, of the excellent progress he is making, nor the extent of the delightful sensations that he awakens in me! And I am careful to keep it that way.

Both of us are finding the roles with which we have been assigned in X—'s play extremely useful with regard to attaining our mutual goal. He is becoming ever more ardent, importunate even. Under the cover of the part he is acting, he is bringing to bear all the very considerable talents with which he is endowed in the attempt to charm and seduce me; I, for my part, sheltering beneath my equally assumed ingenuity (and I should say here that I can play outraged virtue just as well as you can), I can drive him to the brink of despair at the drop of a hat. Whenever I pretend not to understand him, or feign naiveté, he is beside himself.

I have no doubt that he is too quick-witted to be taken in completely, but all the same, I think I have managed to throw him off balance. At the very least he must be asking himself whether he is really dealing with an utter little fool, a thorough-going Agnes, or some mischievous goblin who delights in tormenting him.

Either he does not, or cannot, read my heart, the darling man, or he would have realised by now how much I, too, long for the happy moment when I shall fall into his arms and surrender my lips to his kisses.

But, after all, Albertine darling, one cannot possibly get to that stage without preparing a cushion for one's fall, can one?

Men accuse us of being coquettes and of playing them false, and I suppose they are right. But let them take us as they find us. Good God! Where would we be if our natures were otherwise? What would those same gentlemen think of us then? Is it not right, when all is said and done, that they should pay dearly for something which gives them so much pleasure?

I want Lucien to place the highest price on his victory, and I shall resist him inch by inch. But just think how well he will be rewarded for all the suffering his love for me has caused him! He cannot possibly imagine the multitude of compensations I have in store for him!

I told you at the beginning of this that I had been gathering information on everyone during my long silence. Part of my collection consists of two very peculiar manuscripts which I intend to transcribe for your benefit. First I should tell you how they came into my hands though.

Last Sunday, a number of guests came to visit us such that we had a very lively group around the dinner table. So lively, in fact, that over dessert, the conversation took a rather liberal turn. The lawyer, doubtless in an expansive frame of mind because Rose was serving at the table, regaled us – in that dry, legal manner of his – with a couple of slightly scandalous anecdotes, X— was less tiresome than usual, and Lucien, ever the brilliant raconteur, had the entire table in stitches. When the meal came to an end, the gentlemen, still in fine spirits, lit their cigars and wandered out into the garden where, no longer hampered by the presence of ladies, they could converse as freely as their hearts' desired. At least, such was my understanding of the situation, based on the guffaws of laughter which reached my ears.

Lucien seemed to be the centre of attention. But what could he possibly be saying to them? I was longing to eavesdrop on this conversation, the only question was how to set about this. Suddenly, Lucien took his leave of the merry group for a moment, entered the house, went up to his room, and came down again with a sheaf of manuscript in his hand.

Obviously, a reading was about to take place which would be most unsuitable for chaste ears such as my own. In the interests of not being overheard, the group retired to the end of a small pathway which ran parallel to a tall, thick hedge where, forming a silent circle about the reader, they gave him their undivided attention.

My curiosity could not have imagined a more favourable set of circumstances.

I took my copy of the play we were rehearsing from my pocket and, as if lost in the most profound of dramatic meditations, I made my way stealthily towards the shelter of the hedge, which concealed my presence so entirely that I was able to catch, in passing, fragments here and there of what Lucien was saying.

He was reciting some verse of his composition, but his voice wasn't loud enough for me to make out what he was saying. Thus, I would have had nothing to show for my pains but for the most fortuitous accident.

When he had finished the reading, this newly formed literary society began to discuss the matter, still standing in a circle at the furthermost extremity of the pathway. Lucien, who was busy listening and replying to the comments and praises of his audience, slipped the manuscript, or thought he did, into his pocket. However, through a gap in the hedge, I saw the packet miss the intended receptacle and fall to the ground. Nobody else noticed what had happened. Still immersed in their discussion, the group drifted off until, turning a corner, it disappeared from view.

Like a panther, I pounced on my prey, seizing the object I so coveted, secreting it about my person, and running back to my room with it – I almost said my lair. Once there, I locked the door, and plunged my head into the secret writings of that most wicked of subjects.

The manuscript consists of two parts, intended as a matching pair. One of these, dearest Albertine, we can, knowing all the facts as we do, estimate at its proper worth. Indeed, if I dared, I would congratulate the author on the faithfulness of the picture he has drawn. But if I like this one enormously, the other is far from appealing to me. In any event, I should tell you that the latter is a translation from the literature of ancient Rome and was originally written some two thousand years ago.

Let us hope that fashion has changed considerably in the intervening period. These works will occupy two entire letters from me, which I shall try to send as soon as possible. They are most curious, as you will see for yourself.

Is Madame satisfied now? Does my letter contain enough new information? Have I made good use of my time?

While I await your reply to these questions, my darling Albertine, I send you my hugs and kisses. I shall pray for your promotion. I know what these things mean; after all, I am not a colonel's daughter for nothing.

Your own,

Adèle

PS Just imagine the figure that Lucien cut when he noticed his rather *risqué* manuscript was lost. Fearful it may have fallen into the wrong hands, he rushed about the house in an almost demented fashion. He questioned the servants, now he is reduced to casting searching glances in the direction of the guests. But neither hide nor hair of it have been found! He's looking almost as perplexed as ever today!
Poor boy! How wretched he must feel! How very wicked of me!

Letter XVII: Albertine to Adèle

Paris.

25th June, 18—

My darling Adèle,

What an utterly enchanting letter! I felt as if I had been whisked away to B— and spent half the day with you and all your various guests.

It goes without saying that I await with impatience a copy of the poem which has given your gallant knight so much cause for concern. I am as curious to know the extent of Monsieur Lucien's libidinous imagination as to discover the extent of the claims he can make as a poet.

I am beginning to believe that you have found an excellent tutor for yourself; and I predict that he, for his part, will discover his pupil to be the wickedest little demon ever to have assumed feminine form.

What dangers and exertions you have had to overcome in the interests of your science!

You really must have looked a sight though, perched on the top of your ladder, all hope of solving the mystery of the old barn pinned to the fleeting whim of the moon! I am sorry to say, however, that Mademoiselle Esau will be of little assistance to you in this respect for the simple reason that she left the school three days ago escorted by a strapping horse guard.

Yes, my dear, my successor in Félice's affections is no less than a burly cavalryman. Best of luck to them both, say I. Personally, I'm more than glad to be shot of her.

How that girl wore me out! You should have seen how thin I had become!

Not only that, but her personality, her manners, and her language were all of a kind calculated to cause me offence. And, if that wasn't enough, there was always the risk that she would upset my plans with regard to changes in the management of the school. Now she's gone, thank God! Let that be the end of the subject.

In her absence however, and thanks to the instruction she gave me, I know enough to be able to confirm that Monsieur Prune may remain in England as long as he likes without fear of any increase in his progeny – provided, that is, his chaste other half continues to be satisfied with making love in the manner you observed her doing with her young apprentice. I shall say nothing more on this subject. A couple of lessons from Monsieur Lucien will teach you more about the matter than ten pages of instructions from me. Try to be patient. After all, the precise moment of your initiation depends on you. But don't make the poor boy wait too long.

Now I come to the important part of my letter: my promotion. Things are moving along very nicely, my dear. Barring accidents, before three months are out I should be the new Madame R—.

If you remember my last letter, on the morning on which I wrote it, the gentleman in question still had not screwed up sufficient courage to pop the question. Well, that evening, he invited me in to see him.

With a moderately beating heart, I accepted. He was plainly a man who had decided on a course of action of heroicproportions, but was not quite sure how to put this into practice.

After a rather rambling introduction, during which he tried to excuse himself as best he could over the misunderstanding of the previous day, he launched into a long speech in which all manner of things were garbled together: a funeral oration on behalf of his late wife, an eulogy to my virtue, and a touching description of the mutual happiness to be enjoyed by two hearts united by the bonds of love and affection, etc., etc., etc. Then, mopping his forehead – and not a moment before time either! – he brusquely continued his peroration. In other words, he asked me, in strictest accordance with the rules of etiquette, to become his wife.

I hardly need tell you that I pretended to be surprised – thunderstruck would be nearer the mark. I refused, I raised every conceivable objection (which were all brushed aside, of course), until finally, being alone in the world and with no-one to depend on but myself, I allowed myself to be brow-beaten into giving my consent, upon which note, delirious with joy, he pounced on my hand, which I abandoned to him without resistance, and which, for want of anything better, seemed to satisfy him.

It only remained to fix the date of the wedding. Even on this subject he had to bully me, for, like you, my own feeling is that men can't be made to wait too long or pay too dearly for the thing they desire so impatiently.

After considerable discussion, it was agreed that I would wear the wreath of orange blossom towards the beginning of September.

By that time, my dearest Adèle, you will be well versed

in all of love's secrets, your pretty white teeth will have nibbled away at the fruit of the tree of knowledge until only the core is left, while I, timid bride to be that I am, shall go to the altar as virginal as the Himalayan snow (as Gautier's Mademoiselle de Maupin puts it).

Goodbye for the present. Send me the poems, and don't lose sight of Mademoiselle Rose for a moment. I'm looking forward to finding out how the lawyer gets on with her.

Lots of kisses.

Albertine

Letter XVIII: Adèle to Albertine

B—.

28th June, 18—.

My dearest Albertine,

Personally, I was always sure that you could wrap our late headmistress's husband round your little finger! At the very thought of possessing you, he would have gone through fire and rain.

I am doubly happy, my dearest Albertine, at your news. Your marriage will assure you a position which is worthy of you, and you have now managed to get shot of a girl who, whatever her merits, would sooner or later have ended up compromising you.

I won't write a word more today though. In its place you will find the fragment of ancient literature which I promised to send you. In any event, I have nothing of note to tell you except that our amateur theatricals have been posponed for a few days because of a minor illness. We have had to send out fresh invitations.

Your very own,

Adèle

A CHAPTER FROM PETRONIUS
The Tutor of the Ancient World, as described by himself

'When I went to Asia,' the old man began, 'as a paid officer in the Quaestor's suite, I lodged with a family at Pergamus. I found my quarters very pleasant, first on account of the convenience and elegance of the apartments, and still more so because of the beauty of my host's son. I devised the following method to prevent the master of the house entertaining any suspicions of me as a seducer. Whenever the conversation at table turned on the abuse of handsome boys, I showed such extreme indignation and protested with such an air of austerity and offended dignity against the violence done to my ears by filthy talk of the sort, that I came to be regarded, especially by the mother, as one of the greatest of moralists and philosophers. Before long I was allowed to take the lad to the gymnasium; it was I that directed his studies, I that guided his conduct, and guarded against any possible debaucher of his person being admitted to the house.

'It happened on one occasion that we were sleeping in the dining–hall, the school having closed early as it was a holiday, and our amusements having rendered us too lazy to retire to our sleeping–chambers. Somewhere about midnight I noticed that the lad was awake; so whispering soft and low, I murmured a timid prayer in these words, "Lady Venus, if I may kiss this boy, so that he know it not, tomorrow I will present him with a pair of doves." Hearing the price offered for the gratification, the boy pretended to snore. So approaching him, where he lay still, feigning sleep, I stole two or three flying kisses. Satisfied with this beginning, I rose betimes next morning, and discharged my vow by bringing the eager lad a choice and costly pair of doves.

'The following night, the same opportunity occurring, I changed my petition, "If I may pass a naughty hand over this boy, and he not feel it, I will present him for his complaisance with a brace of the best fighting cocks ever seen." At this promise the child came nestling up to me of his own accord and was actually afraid, I think, lest I might drop asleep again. I soon quieted his uneasiness on this point, and amply satisfied my longings, short of the supreme bliss, on every part of his beautiful body. Then when daylight came, I made him happy with the gift I had promised him.

'As soon as the third night left me free to try again, I rose as before, and creeping up to the rascal, who was lying awake expecting me, whispered at his ear, "If only, ye Immortal Gods, I may win of this sleeping darling full and happy satisfaction of my love, for such bliss I will tomorrow present the lad with an Asturian of the Macedonian strain, the best to be had for money, but always on the condition he shall not feel my violence." Never did the stripling sleep more sound. So first I handled his plump and snowy bosoms, then kissed him on the mouth, and finally concentrated all my ardors in one supreme delight. Next morning he sat still in his room, expecting my present as usual. Well! you know as well as I do, it is a much easier matter to buy doves and fighting cocks than an Asturian; besides which, I was afraid so valuable a present might rouse suspicion as to the real motives of my liberality. After walking about for an hour or so, I returned to the house, and gave the boy a kiss – and nothing else. He looked about inquiringly, then threw his arms round my neck, and "Please, sir!" he said, "where is my Asturian?"

"'It is hard," I replied, "to get one fine enough. You will have to wait a few days for me to fulfill my vow."

'The boy had wits enough to see through my answer, and his resentment was betrayed by the angry look that crossed his face.

'Although by this breach of faith I had closed against myself the door of access so carefully contrived, I returned once more to the attack. For, after allowing a few days to elapse, one night when similar circumstances had created just another opportunity for us as before, I began, the moment I heard the father snoring, to beg and pray the boy to be friends with me again, – that is, to let me give him pleasure for pleasure, adding all the arguments my burning concupiscence could suggest. But he was positively angry and refused to say one word beyond, "Go to sleep, or I will tell my father." But there is never an obstacle so difficult audacity will not vanquish it. He was still repeating, "I will wake my father," when I slipped into his bed and took my

pleasure of him in spite of his half-hearted resistance.
However, he found a certain pleasure in my naughty ways,
for after a long string of complaints about my having cheated
and cajoled him and made him the laughing-stock of his
school-fellows, to whom he had boasted of his rich friend, he
whispered, "Still I won't be so unkind as you; if you like, do
it again."

'So forgetting all our differences, I was reconciled to the
dear lad once more, and after utilizing his kind permission, I
slipped off to sleep in his arms. But the stripling was not
satisfied with only one repetition, all ripe for love as he was
and just at the time of life for passive enjoyment. So he woke
me up from my slumbers, and, "Anything you'd like, eh?"
said he. Nor was I, so far, indisposed to accept his offer. So
working him the best ever I could, to the accompaniment of
much panting and perspiration, I gave him what he wanted,
and then dropped asleep again, worn out with pleasure. Less
than an hour had passed before he started pinching me and
asking, "Eh! why are we not at work?"

'Hereupon, sick to death of being so often disturbed, I flew
into a regular rage, and retorted his own words upon him;
"Go to sleep," I cried, "or I'll tell your father!"'

Letter XIX: Adèle to Albertine

B—.

29th June, 18—.

My dearest Albertine,

It has been raining cats and dogs here all morning – quite impossible to set foot out of doors. Everybody is grumpy. I have shut myself in my room and this time I send you an example of modern literature. I am quite sure you will like it more than the other one.

Your very own,

Adèle

A Stormy Night

They gaze upon each other, and their eyes
   Gleam in the moonlight, Eulalie's arm clasps
Round Anaïs's head, while hers about Eulalie lies
   Almost lost in the tresses which it grasps.
'Tis a sultry August night; the stars, like spies,
   Record the couple's every move, their gasps,
Their sighs, photographing them in pose antique,
Half-naked, loving, unnatural and Greek.

Yet this is a respectable home, not one reviled,
   No house of ill-repute, lust and debauchery.
Mother and daughter live here, or so they're styled,
   Eulalie, svelte, brunette, a woman of thirty three,

Anaïs, the younger, pretty, dimpled and fair, a child.
  Lascivious scenes such as these happen nightly,
Sights which might arouse a Lazarus for a season,
God knows, even make St Anthony see some reason.

No maternal ties bind this union steeped in vice,
  But a sordid transaction of commercial kind.
For Anaïs Eulalie exchanged the market price,
  Though cheap the bargain for one divine
Who would satisfy all her carnal appetites
  And could be trained virtually by design.
Strange to tell, this affair of hawk and dove
Was based on – well, some might have called it love.

As our restless tribades slumber amidst the teaming city
  Beset by the myrmidons of the law, the gutter press
With its screams of scandal, the latest sordid mystery
  Unveiled, a sudden movement reveals their distress.
Could it be that surrounded by such troubling chastity
  Each dreams of a masculine caress?
But if propagation of the species is, for some, a pleasure,
It is one that women such as these may repent at leisure.

Letter XX: Albertine to Adèle

Paris.

3rd July, 18—

My darling Adèle,

You are quite right: *A Stormy Night* is infinitely preferable to *A Tutor of the Ancient World*. Although technically accomplished, the fidelity of the translation, in my estimation, makes neither the content nor the form a jot more appealing.

I don't know whether it is a matter of female sensibility or personal disinclination, but I have never been able to feel anything but revulsion when I think there are men on the loose who seek out such vile pleasures. Ugh!

I am quite vexed with your Lucien! Why bother to dig up such unpleasant characters from the past! Is it not better to leave such turpitudes to slumber undisturbed in the pages of an old book? Nothing less than the graceful pictures he provides for us of Mademoiselle Eulalie and Mademoiselle Anaïs would have earned my forgiveness. Their faults, such as they are, are entirely comprehensible. Alas, poor girls that we are, whom nature has endowed with desires as impetuous as those of any man, yet who have also been denied the chance to concede to the sensuous demands of our momentary impulses by the risk of falling into shame and poverty; are we so much to be blamed for seeking in each other's arms similar pleasures which, however imperfect they may be, are at least free of incessant worry?

How's that for a sentiment which must certainly have been inspired by some eighteenth century philosopher whom I must have stumbled over without noticing. Please forgive me for it, and let me say that I think Monsieur Lucien is a monster of indiscretion. It is not at all a gentlemanly thing to do to steal a woman's secrets and then broadcast them to the world. I hope you give him a scolding on my behalf – but only when, of course, you are in a position to do so. Is that very far off?

I must leave you now, though I have not told you half of my news. But the duties of running my school beckon me. I am introducing all manner of reforms. My future husband leaves me entirely in control, and is content just to watch me with adoring eyes. Things are really looking up.

Goodbye, Adèle, darling. Try and write to me soon.

Albertine

Letter XXI: Adèle to Albertine

B—.

5th July, 18—.

My dearest Albertine,

Maître J— has won his case! He has been most impressive throughout the trial. Rose surrendered last night after a heroic defence… Let us honour her bravery in defeat!

Although I was not present for the hand to hand fighting, I heard enough to be in a position to write an entirely impartial account of the struggle.

Guessing that the drama was reaching its dénouement

for these last few days, I have not missed a single gesture made by either of the leading actors.

Yesterday, about the time Rose normally tidies the lawyer's room, I took up my post at my right hand spy hole where, comfortably ensconced, I bided my time.

I hadn't been waiting for more than five minutes when in came learned counsel, just as I had expected.

The pair of them soon began to talk most earnestly, though I had the greatest trouble in following what they were saying as they both spoke in what was little more than a whisper.

The seducer was determined to triumph at any cost, dangling beneath her nose all manner of promises. From time to time words such as 'perfume', 'apartment', 'dresses', and 'cashmere', reached my ear, exploding like incendiary bombs. How long could Rose hold out against an offensive like this?

And, in fact, I could see her defences weakening. The beautiful young girl, with eyes lowered and a voice which was breathless, was only resisting for the sake of form and her reputation. When Maître J— took out a wallet furnished with a thick wad of banknotes and gold coin, and let her squeeze it between her fingers, all serious resistance was over. A rendezvous was arranged for the same evening.

But where and when? I missed that bit.

Would the lawyer go to Rose, or would Rose go to the lawyer? Would they meet for the first time on neutral ground? That's what I failed to catch.

The little man, standing on tip-toe to do it, planted a

big kiss on her lips, which were as red as peonies, as if to seal their deal. Then he slipped away like a sylph in order not to give rise to any gossip.

Nothing further occurred during the rest of the day.

My God! How interminably the day must have dragged by for Maître J—! He was like a cat on a hot tin roof. He couldn't sit still for a moment, bounding out of his chair, pacing up and down, pulling out his watch, mopping his brow!

Thankfully, the day at last drew to a conclusion and everybody retired to their rooms. More expectantly than ever, I resume my station...

The lawyer is awaiting the bewitching hour before making a move. Meanwhile, he strides back and forth in his room like a caged tiger.

Eleven o'clock strikes. Nothing happens. The house still hasn't settled down for the night. Half past eleven sounds. Still nothing. My neighbour undresses and gets into bed. Evidently, the rendezvous is to be in his room then!

Midnight! He sits bolt upright in his bed as if activated by a spring. The appointed hour is at hand.

Five minutes pass by. Everywhere is silent, as silent as the grave. The wind makes the tops of the tall poplars sway and the leaves rustle. This is all.

Has Rose had a change of heart? Will she keep her word? I can feel all Maître J—'s fears and anxieties.

Sssh! Somewhere the hinges of a door are creaking. There is the sound, carefully muffled, of footsteps in the corridor.

Quick! Let's see who it is!

The lawyer's door, which he has left ajar, swings open, and Rose comes in, pale and trembling and unsure of herself. But she looks absolutely ravishing in her white nightgown, though her attire does little to hide the generous curves of her figure.

The advocate, clearly overjoyed, wraps his arms around her and pulls her towards him. She tries to resist, and he forces her to sit down on the bed. One last effort and she is there beside him... Now what will happen?

I am all eyes. I feel as if I could see through a wall of solid lathe and plaster...

At that moment disaster strikes!

The candle is snuffed out, everything becomes pitch black. There is not even any chance of the moon coming to my assistance. What can I do? There's nothing else for it but to listen.

And that is what I do.

Rose is sobbing. I can hear her weeping and pleading with him. But without effect. Are the words which seem to get caught in her throat an indication of how much she is suffering? I can't say. In any event, Maître J— seems quite unmoved, and presses on relentlessly with his plan.

Rose's sobs intensify. Suddenly, I hear her cry out, surely in pain.

Then there is silence... Everything is over.

What a monster! How dare such a man prey on women like that! Wait a second though. Now he is hugging his victim, offering her all manner of comforting words. Gradually, she calms down and stops

crying... Surely that wasn't a laugh of hers? They are whispering together. I can't make out any of the words properly. Is that the end of it? Might I as well go back to bed? I almost feel like it.

Ah-ha! The lawyer is getting restless again. There is more discussion, another show of opposition, but this time he overcomes it easily. There is no cry of pain now, just some faint sobs which are smothered by kisses. Then there is a very long silence, and that is all.

By this stage I was exhausted through lack of sleep. I hoped to wake up as soon as it was light and succeed in witnessing the part of the performance I had missed.

Do you really think, my dear Albertine, that I could close my eyes for a moment? I tossed and turned in my bed restlessly. Despite myself, I still had one ear pricked up.

Hearing absolutely nothing, I eventually nodded off though. I have no idea how long I had been asleep when I was awakened by the sound of a door being carefully opened.

In a flash I was back at my peephole. The lawyer was alone in bed; Rose had slipped back to her own room. It was four o'clock in the morning. I was too late!

The next day the girl's haggard appearance (her eyes were puffy, her complexion quite pallid, and it was as much as she could do to drag herself from one domestic chore to the next) was in stark contrast to that of Maître J—, with his beaming countenance and air of swagger, who ate a hearty breakfast and swilled down all the coffee and orange juice he could lay his hands on.

Goodbye for now, my darling Albertine. I am looking forward to the return match, even if it means I have to stay up all night.

Your very own,

Adèle

Letter XXII: Albertine to Adèle

Paris.

7th July, 18—.

My darling Adèle,

I have not had a moment to spare these last few days, yet how could I possibly leave your last letter unanswered? My heartfelt congratulations! You would make a first rate historian! Everything is there, not a detail missing!

I have been able to follow the misdeeds of that monkey of a lawyer of yours as if I was hard on his heels. Just imagine what you would have found to write about if the candle hadn't gone out at the moment it did!

But still, the next match has only been postponed, not cancelled. I know what a lynx-eyed little spy you are, and I am looking forward to hearing your complete account in the near future of what Lucien might describe as their 'crimes unveiled".

On that subject, what has become of your Lucien? I trust that the day of his triumph is at hand. It's been more than a month now that you have been systematically refused to accord him the very thing that you can't wait to give him! Enough is enough! Honour is satisfied! I beg you to spare him; more to the point, I beg you to spare both of you. If you are only waiting for my consent before consummating the union, I send it to you freely, together with my blessing. Try to make good use of it.

The school has accepted – or, rather, since I now interview the parents, I should say 'I have accepted' – a new border. I will tell you all about her in my next letter. For the moment you'll just have to make do with the information that she's seventeen years old and that she is utterly exquisite. Unfortunately, she will be only spending a couple of months at the school before leaving to get married.

On that note, I send you my hugs and kisses. Don't be vexed with me for writing such a short letter – I promise that my next will be much longer.

Albertine

96

Letter XXIII: Adèle to Albertine

B—.

18th July, 18—.

My dearest Albertine,

You were quite right: the match was not cancelled, just postponed. What a complete revenge I have had over that blown out candle! This time I have seen everything there is to be seen. Nothing is hidden from me any longer. The veil has been lifted! Day has dawned! All that is left for me to do is to capture as faithfully as a photographer the scene which unfolded before my very eyes, and I can assure you that this will be no easy matter.

You congratulate me on how detailed was my last letter to you. Good God! It was not difficult: it was just like taking shorthand. I listened and I wrote down what I heard. But this is of a different order of magnitude. I could hardly believe my own eyes when I saw what I saw, so how can you expect me to describe it to you so vividly that you will feel as if you were actually there at the same time?

Anyway, I hope you will bear with me and I have every confidence in your perspicacity. Let's pick up the story at the moment I left off.

The day after the dramatic revelations occasioned by that first rendezvous, the theatre was closed. One can understand that in view of the stresses and strains, not to mention emotional exhaustion, that the leading lady must have felt after such début. She richly deserved a short break.

The following night, there was a repeat performance of the first night, but without all the pathos. Rose was becoming inured to the role. Despite my fine resolutions, I woke up in the morning again just in time to see Maître J—, alone by this time, roll over towards the bolster.

You can't imagine how angry I was! And for good reason, as I am sure you will agree! That evening, by way of consolation, I was able to watch my neighbour get ready for bed. But five minutes after his head touched the pillow, he was snoring fit to shake the foundations. With him it's a bit like the Opera: performances are on alternate days only.

So yesterday the theatre was in action. I polished the lens of my opera glasses and I waited.

The auditorium was as bright as day; the lawyer, contrary to previous performances, remained standing in his dressing gown.

Something out of the ordinary was obviously on the cards.

At midnight, the sanctum opened and the goddess appeared in all her radiance. The lawyer dashed over to her, grabbed her hands, kissed her, and dragged her towards the bed. There, despite her protests, he gently but forcibly removed, one after the other, her petticoats and her bodice, which were the only garments she was wearing, such that within the blink of an eye she found herself as naked as Eve before the Fall.

Her blonde tresses, which had accidentally come undone, and which reached down to her waist, only served to make her impersonation of the mother of the human race seem all the more convincing.

What a sight was offered to the bemused gaze of our friend the lawyer.

One might easily have imagined that one of those larger-than-life characters that the vigorous brush of Rubens so delighted to paint had stepped down from the canvas.

Though it could not be said that her limbs were as perfectly shaped as those of my aunt, nor that her hands and feet display the same delicacy, nor that her carriage has the same upright quality, nonetheless she is a very fine figure of a woman. What hips and shoulders! Her legs and thighs look as if they had been sculpted in marble, like the pillars of a temple! And her flesh is so firm and elastic! Despite their considerable fullness, her breasts jutted out proudly, their rosy points remaining parallel to the ground!

The lawyer had likewise cast off his mortal mien, he was more like a satyr – though minus the cloven hoofs and the horns. He roared his approval; he ran his hands convulsively over her body; his lips followed hard on his wandering hands, leaving the imprint of his kisses wherever they had strayed. Like the wicked ogre in a fairytale, he plunged himself head first into a drunken orgy of firm young flesh!

But these preliminaries did not suffice him for long. Faced with such a ravishing Eve, he soon wanted to enjoy the same prerogatives known to Adam. Tearing off his dressing gown, he, too, quickly presented himself in the same state as that which he was born. But how can I describe to you what I saw next, my darling? What I witnessed dumbfounded me, though I might lack the words to express my amazement. Right before my very eyes I saw rear up the living equivalent of that instrument, which it turns out is but a feeble reproduction of the real thing, with which my aunt is wont to console herself.

What an enormous fig leaf would be required to allow Maître J— rights of audience (with any decency, at least) before a justly incensed God!

Now I could understand the reason why Rose had groaned in the way she did; an object half the size would have been cause for concern.

I am sure you are laughing as you read this, my darling Albertine, because you imagine that Maître J— is an ugly devil and quite grotesque in his way. But no, suddenly his ugliness had disappeared. His eyes sparkled, his nostrils flared, his entire face and body reflected the energy and passion which burned within him, and which had completely transformed him. Indeed, he looked almost handsome like that. I found that he aroused two conflicting emotions in me: a sort of desire mingled with terror.

I must admit to you that I was at the stage where I observed his victim almost enviously!

As for Rose, though still protesting and being forced to do as she was told, she was now stretched out on the bed, revealing all the most intimate secrets of her beauty to the lingering gaze of her persecutor.

At the sight of these hidden charms, the little man's fury knew no bounds. He threw himself frantically across this altar, like a soldier going into battle, against which he pressed his head tightly for what seemed like an eternity.

Rose had forgotten all about her tears and protestations. Ripples of voluptuous pleasure surged through her body. Every expression of delight known to the French language issued from her half open lips; and when, abandoning his somewhat unorthodox posture, the courageous little lawyer, more hardy than ever, arose to consummate the ultimate sacrifice, she resigned herself without flinching to the instrument of her martyrdom, and did everything she could to welcome it.

The performance ended and the theatre emptied.

Did the actors rest on their laurels? Did our learned friend Maître J— provide an encore?

I did not bother to find out. I no longer felt the least desire to watch. What I needed to do was to relieve as best I could the terrible thirst for pleasure that had been aroused by what I had seen. It was no longer blood which circulated in my veins but fire!

Ah, if only Lucien had been there! Alas, he was not; and I was left to my own devices.

It is a wise woman, my darling Albertine, who knows how to content herself with so little.

Your very own,

Adèle

Letter XXIV: Albertine to Adèle

Paris.

14th July, 18—

My darling Adèle,

Please believe me, my dear, that no-one can have been more conscious than I of all you must have suffered during your solitary confinement.

You have been subjected to nothing less than the torments of Tantalus, alone in your bed like that, knowing that such a fascinating duet was being performed just the other side of a flimsy partition wall. My heart goes out to you.

If only I had been there, I might have been able to do something to alleviate your agonies – though, and let's be quite honest about this, you did bring a fair amount of it on yourself.

In fact, if you had listened to my advice, it would never have happened at all. It's your own stupid fault for leaving Lucien dangling on a string. You could have avoided the entire situation if you had just shown him a little pity.

If you had treated him differently, instead of being a solitary spectator, you would have had your very own knight errant at your beck and call, a luxury which has now been denied you.

Indeed, when the curtain came down in the next room, the duet might easily have grown into a quartet – and how many encores would you have sung then! Given your reluctance to allow matters to take their natural course, you have only yourself to blame for the terrible boredom, frustration and loneliness about which you complain so bitterly now.

You must learn your lesson and mend your ways!

I must confess though, my dearest Adèle, than in any other circumstances, your portrait – very much in the style of the Flemish masters – of the Junoesque Rose would have inspired me with a desire bordering on the fanatical.

How opulent her figure, how smooth her body! It makes your mouth water to think of her! How one would like to just eat her up!

But, unfortunately, at the moment all my faculties are focused on a sole object of desire. My plans have but one goal. I have fallen head over heels in love with one of our new pupils, Jeanne de K—, and I have eyes only for her. She is absolutely divine.

If Rose represents the triumph of the flesh, Jeanne, on the other hands, is the living incarnation of the poetic ideal.

Her magnificent hair, which glints with gold, crowns her forehead and falls in silky ringlets over her adorably shaped neck; she has dreamy, blue eyes (not unlike Scheffer's *Marguerite*) fringed with long chestnut eyelashes; her skin is so delicate and white that the least emotion makes it blush scarlet; her svelte body is blessed with rippling curves; her hands are almost diaphanous; and her feet are perfection itself.

More generally, she has a vaporous, other-worldly quality about herself which makes her seem spiritually superior to other mere mortals! One is almost surprised to see her feet touch the ground, and one has to resist the impulse to curtsy before her.

Well, my darling Albertine, I hardly dare admit it even to you, but I am meditating – no, more than that – I have decided upon the fall of this particular angel!

Yes, I want her, I must have her, I *shall* have her! Of course, in the case of failure (for one must anticipate all contingencies), I might well compromise myself here, even lose the position I covet. I realise this, everything tells me this is so, yet it changes nothing for me. I have ears only for the siren-like call which pulls me towards Jeanne – and I do not want to listen to anything which will distract me from this goal!

Have I ever failed in any of my projects of seduction? So why should I fail now? And you cannot imagine with what prudence I intend to proceed!

Would you care for some biographical details, as I am in a position to provide them for you?
Mademoiselle de K——, as her name suggests, is of fine old Breton stock. She lost her mother when she was very young, and her father, being a naval officer, and not in a position to look after her, entrusted her upbringing to a bigoted aunt living in Rennes. Jeanne was raised by this old maid, with whom she remained in unbroken contact, according to the strictest precepts of devotional practice, precepts at once combining the worst aspects of spinsterish narrow-mindedness and the most unforgiveable provincialism! All she has ever heard from her lips is a litany of the names of the Blessed Virgin and the saints.

She imputes the most trivial incident to sin, and willingly accuses herself of:

Having caught a flea while at her devotion,
She did kill it with excessive commotion.

If that was not enough, she is almost indescribably naïve; though even so, she is not without a certain native intelligence, which raises its head at the least expected moments.

The circumstances which led to this budding saint falling into hands such as mine are as follows. The aunt died recently; so the niece and her governess, an Yvonne somebody or other, were immediately packed off to Monsieur de K— , who has now retired from the sea and lives in bachelor quarters in Paris. But he had no idea what to do with a young daughter who seemed to fall out the sky straight into his cabin, and so he, in turn, packed her off to us.

In addition to his daughter, Monsieur de K— is also blessed with a nephew, like himself a sailor, to whom Jeanne has been betrothed since childhood. At the moment he is overseas somewhere, but as soon as he returns, which can't be more than a month or two off, the wedding will take place. I intend to use that time wisely and restore his charming bride-to-be to him in a completely disabused condition. Given her present state of primeval innocence, it would be nothing short of a crime to hand her over to some brutal and ill-mannered sea-dog who is more than twice her age and whom she has set eyes on no more than three or four times in her life. I am sure, my darling Albertine, you will agree that I act from the purest of motives and without the least self-interest in this matter.

As you know, I am completely in charge of the running of the school. Our late headmistress's husband having handed over all authority to me, I rule as absolute sovereign and master of the establishment. Almost from the moment of her arrival, on the pretext that the delicate situation of her marital arrangements made it impossible for her to sleep in the main dormitory, I arranged for her to stay in the large room adjoining my own bedroom. In this way I am separated from her only by a glass door. Thus, like you, I find myself permanently *tantalised* every evening; and, alas, like you, I am called on to make the most of my own resources while awaiting the day on which the heat of my desire melts the beautiful statue which slumbers, cold, chaste and pure, only a few steps away from me. Little by little she is learning to like me; she already has so much confidence in me that she tells me all those girlish little secrets; a few more days and I shall make a further modest advance. Don't worry. I shan't do anything without having first secured my line of retreat. Unlike with Félice, I am sure that this time I must act with the most complete circumspection.

Your very own,

Albertine

Letter XXV: Adèle to Albertine

B—.

17th July, 18—

My Dearest Adèle,

My prayers go with you in your latest venture. St. Jeanne is a conquest worthy of you, and I entirely approve the noble task you have undertaken. The very best of luck to you!

This is nothing less than a labour of love, and you should not try to convince yourself otherwise. You will have much hardship to endure: the sleepless nights, all the exertions of instilling a full education, which must be as varied as it is instructive, the need to repeat the same lesson a hundred times, the thousand minor details which can never be neglected

Of all these things, the future bride-groom will remain blissfully unaware; and even if he were perchance to discover the lengths to which you had gone to turn this girl into the perfect wife, do you think he would feel the least obligation to you?

Men are such ungrateful beasts! Fortunately, the task itself will be reward enough for you. Your conscience will tell you that you have done your duty. Finally, Jeanne, the angelic Jeanne, will always harbour a boundless sense of gratitude towards the woman who initiated her into such exquisite mysteries, the foretaste of the perfect bliss which but few, propelled towards their destination by their own ethereal longings, are privileged to experience! As for my news, B— is quite deserted. We have just lost two of our regular party.

The day before yesterday, Maître J—, after reading and re-reading a letter which arrived during lunch, informed my aunt that urgent business recalled him back to Paris. On that note, he left the table and departed the very same day.

Yesterday, it was Rose's turn to receive a letter which she immediately handed over to my aunt. Her mother is on her death-bed, it would seem, and wanted to bestow her blessing on Rose before she died.

There was no time for delay, as you can imagine, and she likewise set off at once for the train station.

On the strength of this double departure I conclude quite simply that the little lawyer has carried off his prey to Paris, where he will be able to devour it at his leisure in some gloomy den in the rue Breda, a den which he will have had furnished, upholstered and gilded at every seam.

So my theatre is suddenly closed for the holidays, at the very moment the cast was about to put in their greatest ever performance.

Admittedly, I can console myself with the production we are about to mount ourselves. The carpenters have been finishing off their work, for tomorrow, come what may, is the day of our *première*.

The invitations have been sent out, and the audience, which will total some fifty or sixty persons, will consist of our neighbours, both near and far. After the performance, a supper has been organised. It will be a proper party.

If I had time, I would describe to you what I shall be wearing. I have just tried on my dress, which suits me perfectly. Modesty apart, I look quite adorable in it, and I have every hope that Lucien will lose all control of himself. I hope you are satisfied! Please don't scold me again, I have taken pity on his martyrdom, and I have resolved to bring it to an end. His ship, as they say, has almost arrived at port.

I must leave you, my darling Albertine, the stage-manager's bell is ringing for the dress rehearsal. I shall be in trouble if I keep everyone waiting.
Write soon.

Your very own,

Adèle

Letter XXVI: Adèle to Albertine

B—.

20th July, 18—
My dearest Albertine,

There can be no going back now!

As I write to you, Lucien has had everything his heart could desire. Oh, the monster — the adorable monster, you understand — what revenge he has reaped on me in the course of a single night for the slight delay to which I subjected his bliss (as he refers to it)!

You asked me to make a complete confession to you, my darling, and that is just what I intend to do.

But I must tell you from the outset that I have been the plaything of such powerful emotions for three days past now that my head is still in a whirl and I know not where to begin.

I shall start anyway, and perhaps my memory will come back to me as we progress.

If you remember, I took my leave of you last time just as the dress rehearsal was about to start. Well, the rehearsal did, indeed, duly start, and Lucien, as if sensing victory at last after the most arduous of campaigns, acted with such passion, such brio – to employ a term much in vogue with the journalists – that he was quite unrecognisable. In short, he was so utterly convincing in his role as seducer that I forgot the double role I myself was trying to play and could only recall that part I was supposed to be showing the audience. Without being aware of it, my eyes reflected the light which flashed from his own, and our two hearts seemed to beat as one.

With both our souls aroused in this manner, we were inspired in rehearsal. Those present, only our most intimate friends and close family, applauded our every move. X— declared enthusiastically that he had never seen better acting at either the Gymnase or the Comédie–Française.

Lucien was delighted by this unexpected triumph, which seemed to anticipate another beyond all price in his eyes. Personally, rather ashamed at having worn my heart on my sleeve in such obvious manner, I slipped away from all the compliments, pretexting a headache. Locking myself in my room, I relived in my mind's eye every moment of the rehearsal, evoking them one by one. Not that this, of course, prevented me in any way from remaining perfectly unreceptive to the silent entreaties of my handsome suitor, clinging continuously to my aunt's crinolines as I did later, and so placing myself out of reach of his solicitations.

The next day, which proved to be so memorable, was largely taken up with endless preparations, the details of which I shall spare you.

Eight o'clock struck!

Our little auditorium, brilliantly lit, was thronged with spectators in evening dress; behind them, in the corridors and the doorways, anywhere a space could be found, the servants could be seen, both ours and those of our friends and neighbours. In all, there were nearly a hundred people.

Suddenly, there were the traditional three loud knocks.

You can't imagine how scared I was by then: I could feel myself turn white under my make-up. Fortunately, I wasn't on first. This ordeal had fallen the lot of my aunt and Lucien, who soon had the audience in fits of laughter. As my aunt made her exit, I could hear a tremendous round of applause for her, which gave me back some of my courage.

My darling! I spoke too soon! One more scene, and it would be my turn. My legs seemed to turn to jelly. If X— hadn't been standing right behind me, I am sure I would have collapsed. I heard my cue. God Almighty! I could not remember a single word of my part! I turned round to escape, but X— was in the way. He literally thrust me on to the stage.

There I was, face to face with Lucien, in front of the entire audience. I caught a murmur coming from the auditorium, and I thought I heard some of the men mutter to themselves: 'I say! There's a pretty little number!' Lucien's eyes reassured me that this was only the truth. This gave me heart, and my memory came back to me. I began to speak. My voice, low and hesitant at first, grew stronger; a line spoken without too much affectation won me a round of applause. I began to breathe again. The great pressure, like a mountain weighing down on me, seemed to lift from my chest. From that moment, I made my entrances and exits without the least gaucheness, my tone was assured and, when my big scene with Lucien came round, I found, under the encouragement of his glance, the same inspiration I had felt the day before. Applause burst out everywhere, and we were rewarded with a standing ovation.

Thrilled as I am, my darling Albertine, to describe to you the success of my first venture into the dramatic arts, I am sure that you are more impatient still to hear the intimate details of my other début, which took place a short while later.

Be patient! We're nearly there, I promise you. In any event, as you will soon see, the two events form a matching pair, you can't have one without the other.

This is how the play ends. I have to give a definitive answer, yes or no, to my lover, who has been pressing me insistently. For various reasons, I am unable to do so right there and then. However, as the curtain falls, he should be able to guess my love for him, and his subsequent victory, from the emphasis I place on the last two words I speak on stage: 'Until later!'

Swept along by the situation, unable to control my feelings any longer, and completely overwhelmed by my love for him, I put so much meaning into those final syllables, and my eyes spoke to him so eloquently, that Lucien could no longer harbour any shadow of a doubt as to the reward I had in store for him later that night. After kissing my hand, he stood up, his face radiant with happiness and his forehead glowing. He had just glimpsed the coast of the promised land for the first time.

Now here's something strange! As the moment was approaching at which I was to put into action the promise I had given so freely of my own accord and give myself to the man I loved, I hesitated – no, not hesitated, rather I would have preferred to delay – I have no idea for what reason, the decisive moment. If I could have done so, I would happily have stopped the movement of the clock, whose hands seemed to me to be sweeping on with terrifying rapidity.

When my aunt stood up, indicating that it was time to retire, I instinctively crossed over to her, as if to place myself under her protection. A pleading glance from Lucien immediately recalled the promise I had made to him. There was no going back.

Once I had reached my room, I carefully closed the door on my aunt's side of the house but made sure that the one leading into the corridor was slightly ajar. Then I undressed, snuffed out my candle, and waited.

Time, which had seemed to fly by only a moment ago, now seemed to have almost ground to halt.

Answer that, if you can! I dreaded Lucien's appearance at the very same time that I longed for it ardently; above all, I wanted there to be an end to the suspense which was almost killing me. I sat waiting in the chair, with my ears pricked, and my hand on my heart, as if to muffle the sound it was making. I felt sure that you would be able to hear it beating in the next room.

Finally, the door was gently pushed open. It was Lucien.

Carried away by a spontaneous impulse, I rushed over to him, snaking my arms around his neck, and hiding my face in his breast. My movement was met with a passionate embrace. His lips searched out mine, I felt myself swept off the floor and carried over to the bed.

He was there beside me, holding me in his arms. I could feel his hand restlessly straying over my body. It only stopped when it encountered my own, strategically placed like that of a bashful Venus. He moved it away and I felt as if the pleasure would kill me!

There are, alas, always two sides to any given coin, or so it is said. I soon realised the incontestable truth of this proverb: a sharp pain soon put an end to the languorous torpor in which I had fallen. Lucien was trying to win the crown which is only bestowed on the most fortunate of lovers. What an injustice! While he was trying to pluck the rose, it was I who was being pricked by the thorns! Despite the heroic efforts I made to stifle them, the pain brought a sob to my throat that my lover vainly tried to soothe with his gentle coaxing.

He was sorry to the depths of his soul for the pain he was causing me but, judging from what I felt, he had no intention of leaving his task unfinished, for he gave me not a moment's respite. Nothing less than complete and utter victory would suffice him.

How long this lasted, and how much suffering I endured, is beyond my powers to describe. Suddenly I felt the deepest, most piercing pain imaginable, as if something was being torn within me. I tried to scream, but the sound was dulled by a thousand kisses. After that, I remember nothing else...

When I returned to my senses, Lucien, who was anxious and upset, whispered all manner of loving words in my ear, words inspired by the tremendous passion he felt for me. I hope you don't imagine for a second, my darling Albertine, that I was vexed with him. Not at all. I loved him more than ever, if that is possible. I was his now, part of me belonged to him. Throwing myself in his arms, I began to kiss and caress him as ardently as he kissed and caressed me.

It will not surprise you, I suspect, when I tell you that he was so lacking in delicacy as to take the most shameless advantage of my magnanimity.

Not content with the decisive victory he had just won, he covered himself with countless fresh laurels plucked from my body despite myself, for I must tell you that the pain had by no means abated, quite the contrary. But what could you expect? He was so insistent and so persuasive, and he behaved so gently, that he obtained everything he wanted.

Fortunately, dawn broke, warning him that it was time to retreat lest suspicions be aroused. After that, I managed to snatch some much needed sleep.

It was after nine when I got up. The first steps I took across my bedroom revived some poignant memories of the night before, and when I glanced into a mirror my tired eyes and drawn face recalled the sorry state and fatigued movements of Rose following her encounter with the lawyer. But Lucien, far from assuming the swaggering airs of Maître J—, only showed himself more affectionate and attentive than ever. I could read in his eyes everything he was longing to tell me with his mouth.

My excessive exhaustion was quite naturally attributed to the play, nobody suspecting what had actually happened. However, every time someone glanced in my direction, it brought a blush to my cheeks, without there being anything I could do about it.

Goodbye, my dearest Albertine. It is after lunch now, but it feels as if I were sending you these dispatches fresh from the field of battle.

Your very own,

Adèle

Letter XXVII: Albertine to Adèle

Paris.

23rd July, 18—

My darling Adèle,

So now you know all about it, this most horrid of secrets! How you have suffered! What a savage is your Lucien! But since you can't find it in yourself to be angry with him, I suppose I must do likewise. In any case, I am sure he has planned the most marvellous surprises for you. That is the very least he could do.

By the strangest of coincidences, the night of your *double début* was also the first time that Jeanne was rallied to the flag under my command.

The dear little girl did not have to undergo anything like the cruel ordeal that you did, but if the next day her face remained unmarked by traces of exhaustion and suffering, she was no less confused than you, and she blushed just as readily. There is nothing more amusing than such embarrassment. She did not even dare to raise her eyes. She was like an angel expelled from heaven, shorn of her wings.

As you know, I was looking for a way of reaching my goal without running any risks. This proved more difficult than it sounds, and I had already considered and rejected a whole range of plans when fate handed me what I was after much more effectively than I could have managed matters myself.

While you were in the midst of your preparations at B— to make everyone forget our best loved actresses, which I am quite sure you are capable of doing, we were suffering a veritable heat wave here. About ten o'clock in the evening, the outbreak of flashes of lightning and claps of thunder warned us that a violent storm was approaching. Jeanne and I went to bed. All the lights were out. She was asleep, or so I thought, in her room, while I lay in bed, vainly wracking my brains as to how to bring matters to a head with her without exposing myself to danger. Suddenly, there was the most fearful crash of thunder, and the glass door burst open. Jeanne, wearing only her night-dress, rushed towards my bed, begging me to let her sleep with me because, she said, she was terrified of the storm.

What do you think of that! Fate must have been listening to my prayers!

I hastily moved over to make room for the trembling beauty who slipped in beside me. I said some comforting words to her, and then I gave her a hug. With every new flash and at every fresh peal of thunder, she squirmed closer towards me until she was pressed against me. As her fear increased, I redoubled my caresses.

I leave to your imagination what sort of state I was in, feeling this delightful body quivering against my own while allowing me to explore all its attractions at my leisure. This contact in itself was enough to render me half-distracted. Still not having attempted anything to alarm her, and enthralled by her physical presence, I rested my head on Jeanne's breast. She thought I had been overcome with terror, and tried to put on a brave front for my benefit. After a short rest, during which time I had gathered my thoughts, I decided to make the most of the storm. As the next roll of thunder sounded, I launched a classic attack: my hand seized hold of my enemy's fortress and held on to it despite strong resistance.

'Albertine! What do you think you are doing!' cried out the unfortunate girl, who felt stranded between Scylla and Charybdis.

'What do you mean, my little darling.'

'Look where you hand is...'

'What about it?'

At this moment there was a flash of lightning followed by a peal of thunder. I gripped hold of my prize in such a manner that my hand could not easily be dislodged.

'Please, Albertine. Stop it!'

I pressed a kiss against her mouth.

'Let me go, Albertine! It's very wicked of you! I don't like it!'

Great flashes of lightning illuminated the sky as if to render it asunder. I made no reply, but wrapped my body more tightly than ever around that of the paralysed girl, still caressing her with my hand.

'Oh God!' whimpered Jeanne, who was beginning to lose control of herself. 'What is happening to me. I feel as if my senses are on fire... No, Albertine, please stop!... What bliss... Holy Virgin, forgive me!... Oh, Albertine, you are killing me with pleasure!... Albertine, darling!... Ohh, ohh!'

The words expired on her lips, and her head slumped against my shoulder. She shuddered, sighed, stiffened, and then collapsed in my arms.

My own desires, only momentarily appeased,

rekindled more ardently than ever. I rolled over across Jeanne's motionless body, crying out in desperation. I kissed her full on the mouth, sucking in her breath. Soon, panting with pleasure, completely overwhelmed by my own needs, I allowed myself free reign to satisfy myself by straddling the hips of the girl I had just initiated into our gross worldly pleasures, pleasures which, for her, will represent no more than a temporary expedient until such time as she shall experience those more natural delights which correspond to her own inclinations and ambitions.

This state of blissful exhaustion could not last for ever. Slowly, we opened our eyes and recovered our senses. Jeanne, overtaken by remorse, burst into a flood of tears, and asked God and the Holy Virgin to forgive her for the pleasure which I had just shown her!

The ungrateful jade tried to evade my kisses and wanted to return to her own room, in order to repent at her leisure the enormity of what she regarded as a carnal sin.

The storm had passed by now. There was not the least flicker of lightning nor the faintest clap of thunder for me to call on. What on earth was I to do?

There was only one thing for it. I started to cry more loudly than the tearful beauty herself. I called on God, the Virgin Mary, and all the saints to vouch for the purity of my intentions, and by these means I managed to make her calm down a little. Gradually, I won back her confidence. Then I employed all my rhetorical powers to prove to her that neither of us was to blame, but that chance and the weather were the real culprits. Besides, it should be remembered that:

One can come to terms even with Heaven.

Whether it was my eloquence which did the trick, or the caresses which I did not fail to lavish on her, or whether she was won over by the desires which I had aroused in her, my bashful sinner yielded to the force or reason and inevitably surrendered herself a second time. From then on, my task was made much easier and, by the time we separated in the morning, I had made a willing convert.

Was I not right, my darling Adèle, in assuring you of my future success? All that is left for me to do is to cultivate the natural aptitude of such an excellent pupil! You, too, will do well to make the most of the excellent instruction which you are undergoing – not forgetting to pass on to me what you have learned!

Love and kisses,

Albertine

Letter XXVIII: Adèle to Albertine

B—.

4th August, 18—

My dearest Albertine,

Yes, yes! Lucien has been storing up some of the sweetest presents imaginable for me, and I am writing to tell you what he has been teaching me every day for his knowledge, like his love, seems inexhaustible.

But even as I dip my pen into the inkwell, a cloud has appeared on the edge of a perfectly blue sky, a cloud which paralyses my hand and mind alike.

A letter arrived yesterday from Algeria informing my aunt of the return of her husband accompanied by another young officer, recently gazetted captain.

This young man would seem to have made a most positive impression on my uncle, for he sends us nothing less than a eulogy as to his character, independence, and physical advantages.

There is surely some match-making at work behind all this. As if to confirm my suspicions, last night, in the drawing-room, just after she had finished a polka, my aunt gaily announced, looking at me as she did so, 'Gentlemen! I hope you enjoy dancing. It looks as if we shall be holding an engagement party before the end of the summer.'

I am not sure of the reason for it, but I have been upset ever since those words were spoken.

Lucien did not say a word about it last night, but this morning I found him gloomy and out of countenance. It was too good to last, I suppose. I should have known that.

Until soon, my dearest Albertine. I just feel as if I want to cry.

As always, your very own,

Adèle

Letter XXIX: Albertine to Adèle

Paris.

7th August, 18—

My darling Adèle,

What a dreadful letter to wrinkle the adorable brow of my fair Adèle and deprive me at the same time of all those intimate details I was so looking forward to. How eager I am to follow, if only at one removed, the instruction of your celebrated professor!

For the time being at least, try only to think of the present. Your anxieties may yet prove a false alarm.

In any case, your uncle isn't back yet. All Lucien has to do is declare his intentions and to ask your aunt for your hand.

After all, he would be the first to reveal himself an interested party, and as such he would have incontestable rights. Your uncle would listen to reason. He certainly wouldn't want to force you to marry his captain if you really didn't care for him.

Have courage, my darling little Adèle! Everything will turn out better than you think!

I have so much to tell you about my new convert, but

that had better wait until another time when you are no longer distracted by your own anxieties.

Goodbye for the moment, my darling. Love and kisses.

Albertine

Letter XXX: Adèle to Albertine

B——.

14th August, 18——

My dearest Albertine,

You can't imagine how miserable I am. Would you believe it, but Lucien has left B——! He went off yesterday evening. Now I am obliged to hide my chagrin and hold back my tears. No–one must know what I am going through.

My aunt received another letter from her husband, much more explicit than the last with regard to my future husband. I tried to explain these matters to Lucien, who refused to talk to me about it, especially when I asked him how he intended to conduct himself with my uncle when he returned. After avoiding giving me a clear and categorical answer, even when I pressed him vigorously, he finally informed me in the coldest tone that he was not free, though when I enquired further about what he meant by this, he wouldn't say. And that was all I managed to get out of him. Then he announced that he had no intention of standing in the way of the marriage that was being prepared for me, and that he thought it would be better if he took his leave of us immediately.

Nothing I could do, neither tears nor supplication, would make him change his mind. Now he is gone!

Oh, my dearest Albertine, what if I should never see him again? You can't imagine how I loved him! Why is he treating me like this? I have passed the most dreadful night. I had to bite my pillow in order to stifle my sobbing. I did not even manage to go down to breakfast, as everybody would have noticed how blotched my eyes were.

Goodbye, my dearest Albertine! Pity me. Write to me. Console me. I am in despair.

Your own,

Adèle

Letter XXXI: *Albertine to Adèle*

[The letter from Mademoiselle Albertine in reply to the heartbroken appeal of her friend has been lost or mislaid. We may presume that it contained all the usual words of consolation that women send to each other in such circumstances, accompanied, no doubt, by some rather unflattering remarks as to the lack of probity of men in general and Monsieur Lucien in particular. The reader may easily fill in the gap, which is of no great merit or importance, from his own imagination.]

Letter XXXII: Adèle to Albertine

B—.

20th August, 18—

My dearest Albertine,

Your kind letter really cheered me up. By destroying some of my most cherished illusions, you have forced me to see things in their true light. My mind has been gradually less agitated, and my tears are almost dry. If I still haven't managed to drive away the memory of the man who was, and still is, extremely dear to me, despite the terrible wrongs he has done me, at least I have managed to hide the injury from everyone else. In truth, though, I am afraid that it will be a long time before my poor heart gets over him.

I thought I wouldn't write to you until my uncle returned, which we have been expecting for the last few days now.

Well, now he is back, I can tell you that though I had doubts about how quickly I would start to recover, I managed to pass my test with him without flinching. Although I couldn't bring myself to pretend that I was overjoyed by the present he had brought back for me, at least I managed to play the part convincingly enough of the well-bred young miss who accepts without either repugnance or enthusiasm the first husband which is offered to her.

Oh, my dearest Albertine! How far short of Lucien this suitor falls in every respect! It is not even as if he was that bad looking. He is a great strapping fellow of some twenty six or twenty seven, who goes around trussed up in a uniform. He has fair hair, a florid complexion, and a waxed moustache. In other words, he's what is commonly described as real officer material. If only he wasn't so stiff and formal! And as for his conversation! All I've heard for the last forty eight hours are stories about the garrison and the regiment – and I've no doubt that I shall probably be condemned to listen to nothing else for the rest of my life! When I think of how witty... Well, I had better stop there or I shall burst into tears again, and then I shall start to look old and ugly. All in all, I don't know which way to turn.

By way of keeping myself occupied, I've taken up painting again, which is something I have tended to neglect recently, as you well know.

I would also have liked to make use of my left hand spy-hole, that might have helped me take my mind off things, except that my aunt has re-arranged her apartments, turning the bedroom into a dressing-room, and vice-versa. I can no longer see or hear anything that goes on in the bedroom.

See if I care! After all, nothing can possibly happen here that I don't already know about.

Until soon, my dear friend. I send you all my kisses.

Adèle

PS My uncle is setting about matters in a most militaristic fashion. Within a month at most I shall be Madame la Vicomtesse de S—. (I forgot to mention that the strapping youth has a title.)

Letter XXXIII: Albertine to Adèle

Paris.

28th August, 18—

My darling Adèle,

I am so delighted to see such a marked improvement, my dear. Did my letter really help you see things in perspective? I would be so proud if that was the case. Time also must play a part in the healing process. The important thing is that you are on the road to recovery, and there is no better proof of that than the fact that you are keen to keep your mind occupied.

It was most thoughtless of your aunt to change her sleeping arrangements without consulting you! A single session at your peep-hole might have brought about a complete cure for you!

I suppose that means the 'Uncle' – the false one, that is – will be languishing forgotten in a drawer from now on. He must be feeling rather sorry for himself since his rival, the real uncle, came back.

Personally, if I had a toy like that in my possession, I can assure you that I would make full use of it.

Perhaps I had better explain myself. First, though, I should tell you that it's not me who is getting interested in that 'Uncle' of yours, but – and I know you will hardly believe this, but I swear that it's true – Saint Jeanne!

To be honest, her education hasn't gone entirely according to the plan I mapped out for it. Given the time and energy I have expended on her, this is something of a disappointment. She does her best to follow my instruction, but it is obvious that her heart isn't really in it, and that she obeys me almost in spite of herself. She has other aptitudes, I'm afraid – aptitudes which I am not really qualified to bring out to the full. As for those imperfect pleasures which she shares with me, I am only too afraid that her ghastly sailor-boy will initiate her into the real thing with everything that entails.

The very thought of this exasperates me, and I can only rail at my powerlessness. I have got to the stage where, quite frankly, I regard this man as an odious rival. I cannot resign myself to the fact that he enjoys the quiet possession of a property which I myself would like to make use of. In the dark recesses of my imagination I plot my revenge on him in a manner worthy of Atar–Gull.[1]

I can see you opening your eyes in amazement at this, and wondering if I am entirely serious. Only to a point, I assure you. Just hear me out on this.

At the risk of appearing quite mad to you, let me tell you of the convoluted plan which has been hatching in my brain ever since I heard that 'Uncle' had been put out to grass. I suspect that he might constitute just the

---

[1] Character in the novel by Eugéne Sue of the same title (1831). The title of the English translation gives some indication of the action: *The Negro's Revenge; or, Brulart the Black Pilot* (1841). (Translator's Note.)

thing I need to accomplish the terrible vengeance I harbour in my soul.

Indeed, might not I, with the assistance of your 'Uncle', pluck that flower which our dashing pirate covets so highly, and towards which he already reaches out his hand?

Can you imagine how angry he would be! This is just the way to deal with an enemy: what you can't pillage for yourself, you put to the sword. It's in the nature of warfare.

Unfortunately, 'Uncles' don't grow on trees. The question is how to get hold of one. That and how might one circumvent Jeanne's scruples at the sight of such a peculiar partner.

To these questions, I have no answer.

Ah, if only the gods of Mount Olympus were still among us! I would offer up the most fervent prayer to Venus this very evening: such an accommodating goddess could hardly refuse me the gift of changing my sex, and that way I would have Jeanne just where I wanted her!

I can see you shrug your pretty little shoulders in despair at such a hare-brained scheme, so I shall stop here.

Until very soon, Madame la Vicomtesse. I send my love and kisses.

Albertine

Letter XXXIV: Adèle to Albertine

B—.

2nd September, 18—

My dearest friend,

This evening, or tomorrow morning, you will receive a little parcel which I am sending by rail. I hope you will be pleasantly surprised by the contents. It is sometimes said that gifts are the very cement of friendship. If this is so, accept this one, and always love me as much as I love you.

Your own,

Adèle

Letter XXXV: Albertine to Adèle

Paris.

7th September, 18—

My darling Adèle,

I cannot thank you enough for your charming present, and nor can I even begin to describe how dumbfounded I was when I received it.

In any event, I am sure you can picture my amazement just as vividly as if you had been there yourself. This is what I did. When I received your package, I carried it into my bedroom. I removed the wrapping paper and found the prettiest little box inside. I opened the box. And there I was rooted to the spot, mouth agape, eyes wide open with astonishment!

What on earth could it be? I lifted it from the velvet lining in which it nestled and examined it closely. I turned it round in my hands, looking at it this way and that. Then all at once I remembered a passage in one of your letters in which you had described it to me, and I realised that this must be your aunt's particular friend, your uncle's stand-in! In short, this must be the instrument I discussed in my last letter, though at the time I knew no more about it than a Dutchman knows about mountain climbing. Talk about giving me a shock! If you're going to give someone a surprise, this is the way to do it! I was utterly ravished!

Only one thing worries me, my little darling. What will your aunt think – and, more to the point, what will she have to say about it? Won't she suspect something? In fact, how did you possibly manage to appropriate her precious talisman?

While I await your reply to these intriguing questions, you should congratulate yourself on your work. Your envoy has been welcomed with the most extraordinary show of enthusiasm. He is the living incarnation, in body and spirit, of all my girlish dreams. What's more, he is ideally suited to the task I have in mind for him.

You may easily imagine the circumspection with which I have surveyed the land, all my uncertainties and irresolution, the infinite precautions I have taken prior to my declaration of war and the uncovering of my heavy artillery. What is less conceivable though – and even you will have to admit the truth of this (to be honest I can hardly believe it myself) – is that, once her initial astonishment had subsided, I found that I had on my hands a pupil whose eagerness, inquisitiveness, and hunger for knowledge surpassed all my expectations.

It is as if a revolution has taken place!

Jeanne, who has always appeared so undemonstrative to me, who always seemed so reluctant to reciprocate the desire I feel for her, as soon as she knew, or rather guessed, the mode of employment of this jewel, which I hardly dared reveal to her, was the first to volunteer her services. The considerable risks associated with such a venture seemed to leave her indifferent. If anything, the contrary was true: she seemed attracted by the danger, almost fascinated by it.

I did not hesitate for a moment. I transformed myself at the drop of a hat into the passionate lover and, with the able assistance of 'Uncle', I stepped fearlessly on to the floor of the area, armed to the teeth. I must admit to you, however, that my lack of experience in this kind of combat was a tremendous handicap to me during the preliminary skirmishes. The least sign of resistance from Jeanne would have led to the utter abandonment of a mission undertaken in such a rash manner. But far from acting as a brake to my enthusiasm, she did everything in her power to encourage it. The pain mingled with the pleasure seemed to spur her on. Her excitement communicated itself to me. Finally, with the assistance of a liberal application of cold cream, I overcame all the difficulties and surmounted every obstacle.

Fascinated beyond measure by the role I had assumed, I lost all affinity with my own sex. The suffering I

inflicted on Jeanne, her screams and groans, the desperation of my lunges and parries, by which I tried to abridge her ordeal as far as possible, all this, far from moving me to pity, provoked in me the strangest feelings: the voluptuous pleasure of exercising my power over her.

Truly do I now understand why men attach such importance to their conquests – the greater the pain they cause, the more they revel in their victory!

What more can I tell you, my darling? I achieved my goal, and I am content. The sailor can call whenever he likes, but the wheat has been harvested. There is still plenty of raking to be done, so let him rake away to his heart's content. I will not make the slightest objection.

As for 'Uncle', whose indispensable aid allowed me to enter into the complete and total possession of Jeanne, he does not look in the least the worst for ware: he is still ready for action at a moment's notice, and remains the most upstanding soldier in the platoon, showing not the slightest sign of either limpness nor fatigue. Certainly, he has every reason to be proud of his resilience under fire, but it would not seem to have gone to his head.

Goodbye for the present, my darling Adèle. How can I possibly thank you enough for the present you have made me?

Albertine

Letter XXXVI: Albertine to Adèle

Paris.

Evening.

7th September, 18—

My darling Adèle,

It transpires that your envoy arrived in the nick of time! A moment's delay, and all would have been lost. Hardly had I sent off my letter to you this morning recounting the famous victory I had won, when Monsieur de K— dropped in at the school out of the blue. His nephew, it would seem, has already left Brest.

Jeanne will leaving me the day after tomorrow. She will be married almost the same time as us.

Which still leaves us two nights together! I shall try to make the most of them: it feels like the end of our adolescence for both of us.

Albertine

Letter XXXVII: Adèle to Albertine

B—.

12th September, 18—

My dearest Albertine.

Nothing could have given me greater pleasure than providing such timely, not to mention efficacious, assistance to you. Quite apart from anything else, I am delighted that you have managed to discover your charming pupil's true vocation. But since her imminent departure leaves 'Uncle' once again without gainful employment, could I ask you to be so good as to return him without delay? I shall put him back where I found him, and my aunt, who has been extremely busy recently, will never suspect my tiny indiscretion.

I must tell you, my darling, that my wedding preparations are progressing at a rate of knots. If you could only see the pretty basket of wedding presents which arrived for me from Paris this morning! Everything was in the best possible taste, and must have cost a pretty penny.

[At the risk of disappointing our lady readers, we shall excise the laborious description of the contents of this basket from our narrative: it runs to two densely packed pages of the most minute script imaginable. As for the gentlemen, I am quite sure that their approbation is obtained in advance.]

I was decidedly mistaken about the Vicomte de S—. Indeed, I will confess to you that he is beginning to please me immensely. As a man, of course, he is extremely handsome. Though he may want for distinction in other departments, though he may still seem uncomfortable in civilian clothes, he looks magnificent when dressed in his full regimental uniform. Not only that, but his conversation, which used to bore me to tears, has undergone a most happy transformation.

As we have grown to know each other better, he has confided in me how uncomfortable he felt during our first meetings. My poor dashing hero is without the least courage in the presence of ladies, and he was completely at a loss to know what to do when faced with my rather sullen attitude towards him. But now that his awkwardness has left him, I take the greatest pleasure in his company. All the same, though he might pass muster in a crowd, he will never win honours for himself as a brilliant conversationalist, and I would not try to convince you otherwise. For my part, I have gradually cast off my rather shrewish temper. Apart from heaving the occasional sigh at his memory, I have slowly forgotten Lucien. If I still behave a little formally towards my official suitor, everybody attributes it to my excessive shyness.

He, on the other hand, is all on fire. He is indefatigable when it comes to organising the marriage and seeing to all the preparations. He spends most of his time on the road between Paris and B—. My uncle and aunt are actively encouraging him. Personally, I have no wish to oppose such haste, quite the contrary. In principle, the ceremony will take place without delay on 22nd September.

Just between ourselves, my dearest Albertine, this is not a moment too soon. I am in the same situation as Bluebeard's sister-in-law: I see nothing coming!

Farewell for the moment. I will probably not find time to write again until after my marriage. But what about yours? You've told me practically nothing!

Your own,

Adèle

Letter XXXVIII: Albertine to Adèle

Paris.

16th September, 18—

My darling Adèle,

I can quite appreciate the urgency of the matter. You are quite right to press forward with the celebration of your nuptial vows.

What a fortunate man, the Vicomte! Whatever happens, he for one will not die without issue! In that respect, at least, Jeanne's husband might well envy yours – always providing, of course, that he doesn't notice that most of the work has already been done for him! I don't want him filing a complaint against me for the excessive zeal with which I have prepared his bride for the marital state. Men can be such unpredictable creatures!

In your case, I have every confidence in your talents as an actress to allay any fears your husband might harbour. If ever there was a time to put such talents to good use, this is it!

Your wedding presents sound magnificent, my darling, and your bridegroom has behaved most handsomely by you. There is much to be said for such a man, and I trust you will reward him well and soon forget all about Lucien.

If I haven't mentioned my wedding, it is for one very good reason: there is nothing to say about it. I drift steadily towards my chosen goal. Nothing untoward or unforeseen can possibly occur. I can tell you quite frankly that the gentleman in question knows not in which register to sing his paeans of love. He has reached the stage of religious adoration or primitive fetish worship. Any day now I expect him to set up an altar to me and burn incense at it. Faced by all this, I behave with admirable sang-froid. With the best will in the world, I can assure you that I do not feel at all equal to such devotion. I won't deny that my future husband is beginning to inspire a certain affection in me, but no matter how carefully I study the matter, I cannot find it within myself to feel anything which bares the slightest comparison to what I felt when I was with you or Félice.

For the last three months, I suppose I have employed my time in such a way that it has absorbed all my amorous energies, and I have not the resources to harbour two great passions at the same time. Indeed, since the departure of my darling Jeanne, I have not permitted myself the slightest distraction. Every evening, I have accustomed myself to listen to the murmur of his words and to allow him to stroke me, I have even steeled myself to let him touch me in a manner which I find irritating rather than the contrary, yet during all this time I have remained cold and frigid.

It is not that the gentleman is past the age at which one can inspire love, he is still a fine looking man in his way, I know all that, I am just unable to reciprocate his feelings. This is what is really odd though: as soon as I retire to my own room, and get into bed, your beloved image, and that of Jeanne, flit about my bedside, pestering me without mercy, and then there's nothing for it but to pay the appropriate tribute due to the indescribably erotic memories I have of you.

Be fair to me, my darling Adèle, I have done my best. It's too strong for me, my heart isn't in it. Whatever the underlying problem, I shall also be married by the end of the month.

Goodbye for the moment. Chaste fiancée that you are, I kiss your forehead!

Albertine

Letter XXXIX: Adèle to Albertine

B—.

25th September, 18—

My dearest Albertine.

I am married! Everything went as well as it possibly could. My maidenly fears had such a genuine air about them, I made such a pretence of only yielding in the face of overwhelming odds, I simulated the pain of defloration so convincingly, that not the shadow of a doubt has crossed my husband's mind.

My triumph was so complete that in the midst of his transports of delight, even as he showered me in kisses, my husband cried out: 'Adèle, my angel. You have made me the happiest man alive!'

Poor fellow! What a trick I have played on him! I swear to you, I feel quite guilty about it. But what choice did I have? I did it for his own best interests. I do love him most profoundly, you see.

What courage it took to stifle the feelings I harboured for him, to repel my own natural inclinations, to fight against his desire for me which was no less strong than my desire for him!

I would like to give you a more detailed account, my dear, but I am no longer mistress of my time. I cannot shut myself in my room as I used to do. I have a lord and master who has the right to penetrate my inner sanctum at any moment and ask me to account for my least action. I make the most of my tyrant's fleeting absence to scribble you these lines.

We return to Paris next month. We shall find time then for me to recount to you at leisure all the things I have left unsaid here.

Until soon.

Your own,

Adèle

Letter XL: Albertine to Adèle

Paris.

8th October, 18—

My darling Adèle,

Just like you, I find myself in possession of a husband; unlike you, however, or so appearances would lead me to believe, he is not yet entirely under his wife's control.

I didn't want to write to you straight after my wedding while I was still affected by feelings which, I am forced to admit, were by no means agreeable to me.I was looking forward – after all, a change is as good as a rest – to

reading the chapter – the famous chapter which you read with Lucien from beginning to end – on the consolations of love. Alas, my dear, I am still looking forward to reading it. Either my husband doesn't know how to console me, or else the deep respect he professes to feel for me prevents him from sullying my angelic purity with those experiences which might accommodate me rather better than all the praises that he continually lavishes on me.

Truth be told, I have reached the limits of my knowledge, however considerable the efforts I have expended on acquiring it. I am also bound to admit that my ·rebellious nature will not allow me to bow down before that pleasure which makes other women so happy.

I would be on the verge of desperation had I not other consolations to look forward to, consolations which have never failed to delight me so far, and which are not without a certain merit in their own regard. Would you not agree with that?

When you return to Paris, my dear little girl, we will talk over these matters in detail.

I look forward to seeing you soon. I send you all my love.

Albertine

Letter XLI: Adèle to Albertine

B—.

12th October, 18—

My dearest Albertine.

We leave B— this evening.

My first visit tomorrow will be to see you. I insist that you put aside the whole day for me. After more than six months apart, I can hardly ask for less, can I?

I am scribbling this note to you in the midst of all my trunks and hat-boxes. I shall post it immediately so as not to take you entirely by surprise.

Be warned! I shall completely monopolise you! So make your preparations accordingly.

In the meanwhile, I send you my love and kisses.

Adèle

Conclusion

With this, the forty first letter, the correspondence of these two young ladies draws to an end.

Their marriages in no way disturbed the perfect harmony which had always reigned between them. They continued to communicate to each other in the most scrupulous fashion the diverse experiments they called upon themselves separately to undertake. But with this difference. Since they no longer used the postal services to act as intermediary between themselves, it is beyond the power of the present editor to offer any further examples of this intriguing exchange.

In the event, however, that the reader might have taken some slight interest in those letters I have been so fortunate to publish, I am able to prove some further information, garnered from the most unimpeachable sources, which throw some light on the subsequent careers of the principal characters who appear in this correspondence.

Madame la Vicomtesse de S— remains as seductive and charming as she reaches womanhood as she was gracious and adorable in childhood. After three years of marriage she has still not entirely fallen out of love with her husband. The Vicomte dotes on his wife and upon the fine son which she bestowed on him after their marriage. He is, or so the Vicomte claims, the spitting image of himself!

Despite all her efforts and good resolutions, Albertine R— has never entirely succeeded in reconciling herself to the more orthodox manner of love–making. She remains something of a heretic in this regard, and has been unable to prevent herself from demonstrating a marked predilection for those of her young charges who have a pretty face combined with a figure indicative of their incipient womanhood. The Pensionnat R— enjoys a reputation as one of the best schools in Paris, and it is widely believed that the young girls who attend it receive an education which is second to none.

Colonel M— and his wife are as much in love with each other as when they went on their honeymoon. More fortunate than Albertine, Adèle's lovely aunt has renounced the cult of all false gods.

Discreetly concealed in his place of retirement, 'Uncle' can rest upon his laurels.

Lucien has enjoyed considerable good fortune since his adventure at B—. Yet even he would admit that he has never met anyone to compare with Adèle. Having chanced across her in polite society, he tried to renew their acquaintance. She, however, replied with a smile that she was no longer free. Lucien took her at her word.

Since her marriage to her cousin, the beautiful Jeanne de K— has succeeded:

Between the true and the false make a discrimination

She often repeats to herself the celebrated line of Boileau:

Only the true is beautiful and fit to love.

She is still, deep down, as devout as ever, and when her husband embarks on one of those perilous expeditions from which his return is entirely in the hands of God, she is a frequent visitor to the Pensionnat R—. On these occasions, she spends many an hour cloistered with her former mistress. Rumour has it that she receives advice in relation to a difficult matter of conscience.

Maître J—, having set up his gorgeous mistress in an attractive apartment, provided so much proof of the violent passions which she inspired in him that, at the very moment it was least expected, he caught some feverish inflammation which carried him off in a week.

Since she became a widow, she has received a host of admirers willing to allow her to cry on their shoulders. But being a sensible girl, and regarding her beauty as her capital, she has been careful to make it yield everything that it is capable of yielding. The product of her labours is duly converted into guilt-edged bonds.

The last time we encountered Félice, the charming girl from Provence was eloping with a cavalryman. She quickly rose through the ranks. As the result of her remarkable features, the strange way she had of looking at men, and certain indiscreet remarks which the trooper himself made with regard to her unusual adornment, she soon attracted the interest of a lieutenant. A captain succeeded the lieutenant, etc., etc. Today, Félice, who works as a dancer, is one of the top attractions at the Mabille, the Château d'Asnières, or the Closerie des Lilas. Everywhere she performs she receives rapturous applause whenever she kicks her leg in the air on a level with her partner's eyes. Her memoirs have proved one of the season's best-sellers.

Is that everyone?

A final word. This is how one of the most delightful poets of the seventeenth century begins one of his stories:

As to talent I make no claim,
  'Tis to the fairer sex I owe my fame.
Thus, the present tale do I dedicate
To gentle readers of all estate.
If false, you will it repudiate;
If true, let it not fail to educate.

Let this beginning serve as our conclusion at the same time as we must bid a fond farewell to our heroines.

Foreword to the 1928 Edition
(illustrated by Jean d'Anger)

The first edition of this short epistolary novel was published in 1868 by Poulet-Malassis, and immediately condemned to destruction by the Tribunal Correctionel de Lille. In our opinion, the severity displayed by these magistrates in their starched collars turned the Law into a laughing-stock – because the Law, especially in France, never loses by being applied with wit and discrimination. And with what indulgence, sympathy even, would not it have been better to treat these mutual confidences of two young girls, extremely well bred as they are, curious, as may be imagined, of the mysteries of love, exercising all their ingenuity to discover how the timeless promises of affection exchanged by couples everywhere is translated into physical action, striving to compute the immensity of that profound bliss by which life itself should be measured...

As is only fitting, their letters are written in the most delicate language, a language which never displays the least vulgarity, and this, combined with the natural zest of the writing, which is at the same time both naïve and lascivious, contributes enormously to their disreputable charm.

Gustave Droz is presumed to be the author of this

delightful work, and there is little which seriously contradicts the likeliness of this traditional attribution. The correspondence of these two young Parisians, however, could just as easily have been written in 1926 as during the most brilliant days of the Second Empire. Men's desires – and women's too – are not subject to a great deal of variation.

This view accords with that of our friend Jean d'Angers, whose gallant sketches succeed better than those of anybody else in illustrating these letters of former times in the light of contemporary artistic tastes. Nothing could be less surprising. What could have possibly changed in the way that we make love?

FIN